Ghost of Time

Cheryl Lawson

Also by the author:

Fiction:

The Rubicon Saga
We Are Mars
Storm At Dawn
Break the Dark

Journey to Vega Novellas
A Dark Genesis
Erebus

Anthologies:

Worlds. Dark Drabbles #1 (Black Hare Press)
VSS365 (2019)

First Published in Canada, 2024.
Published by SW Sci-Fi, an imprint of Southernwood Technologies Inc. 2021.

ISBN 978-1-989872-13-0

Dedication

To David and James

ONE

Sector B3

"Sir, there's something out there."

"Nav, can you elaborate?" The impatient query came from Commander Morris, the officer in charge of the *Vega Two's* second-shift bridge crew.

"Yes, sir. Sorry, sir. I'm just getting more data now," said the navigation officer, Lieutenant Wu. "There appears to be a spatial anomaly intersecting with our flight path that long-range scans only now detected."

"A spatial anomaly?" Commander Morris frowned. "Meaning?"

"Sir, there isn't much data, except that there's a change to the sensors readings for sector B3, bearing approximately eighteen degrees starboard. The gravitational sensors are having trouble calibrating for that sector, and I can't get a fix on measurable radiation."

"I see."

The bridge crew grew quiet, awaiting instructions from the commander, who pondered the latest update from his team.

Lieutenant Lena Dixon watched from her station; her fingers poised over the pilot's controls. The shift had started a little over two hours earlier and she was already tense, her knotted neck and shoulder muscles burning. Morris was a hands-on commander. Every person there had a roster of tasks to complete, and the eight-hour second shift usually flew by as the bridge crew, also known as Command by the rest of the *Vega Two's* occupants, worked.

Lena loved her job, but it was exhausting. She knew that over time, she'd become more accustomed to the long hours and demanding rigor of the shift, but as a new Command recruit, on her fifth bridge rotation, she dragged herself back to her bunk at the end of each day, exhausted and barely able to focus on the assignments she still had to complete for the remaining courses she was enrolled in.

She admired the commander, but she also wished, every now and then, that he'd ease up on them a little.

"Right, maintain course and continue to do sector

sweeps. We need more data to analyze before we bother the captain with this." The commander flopped into the captain's chair, still wearing a frown.

Spatial anomalies were not all that common, and most were nothing more than a gas cloud or a shower of radioactive particles emitted by a star. Sometimes, a course correction was needed. Most times, the *Vega Two* crew simply increased the strength of the shield array and pushed ahead. A lack of data could be an indication that the sensors had detected the barest traces of some or other element, and in the process, triggered an alert at the navigator's station. There was no way to tell without more sensor information.

Lena's attention was soon back on task, and the hours flew by with an almost unnatural speed. At least, that's how it felt to her. Eight hours simply evaporated, and the unexpected shrillness of the bosun's whistle, signaling the end of shift, made her jump in her seat.

"Where did the time go?" she asked Lieutenant Wu, who sat to her left.

"Could have sworn we still had two hours left, but it just went by so fast today. Not that I'm complaining." She smiled at Lena. "I have a Chem final to cram for."

Wu was also finishing her studies at the academy and Lena gave her a nod of comprehension. "Good luck!

Winchell's exams are always tough, but you'll be fine."

"Thanks, Lena. See you tomorrow." Wu walked briskly away in the opposite direction when they stepped off the elevator.

"Boo!"

Lena yelped, her hand flying to her throat. "Jesus, Vince. You scared the crap out of me." A light beeped on a nearby wall panel and Lena sagged against the cool metal, taking the fine issued from the well-worn slot of the etiquette monitor. She waved the blue paper at the object of her annoyance. "Thanks for that," she ground out through clenched teeth.

Her friend, Vince, only laughed good-naturedly before slinging an arm over her shoulder and snatching the paper from her fist. "Ah, Len. The look on your face was worth it." He pocketed the slip on which her offensive language, and the rules it violated, were detailed. Not everyone took the etiquette programs on board the *Vega Two* seriously anymore. Vince counted himself in that number of rebellious souls who thought they were above the rules and regulations. With each new generation of travelers bound for the distant Vega System on board one of several Ark-class ships, the rules of living changed; ebbed and flowed. *Vega Two* was no different from the twenty or so other generation ships taking Earth-origin humans across the vast expanse of the galaxies to a new home.

"You'd better pay it this time, Vince. I almost got a stay in the brig for that last prank you pulled."

"I swear, you have got to relax, Lena." He smiled persuasively at her, his self-confidence always a point of friction for them. She thought he was vain and condescending. He thought he was the best thing to grace the behemoth vessel they lived on. "I will pay your little fine, but you owe me a game of Snag."

"Vince." Lena knew she sounded whiny, but she was tired, and besides, she hated the chase-and-hide game. "I have exams."

"Excuses. That's all I get from you these days." His charming smile faded. "We never hang out anymore."

Lena bit her tongue. She had almost blurted that training to be a bridge officer was a lot harder than learning how to bake bread. Vince was being taught the family business. His family ran the ship's bakery, and with his parents aging out of the work program, it was up to him and his brother to take over. Running the only bakery on the *Vega Two* was important work. She knew that.

"Yeah, sorry, Vince," she finally managed. They'd slowed and were standing near one of the large potted trees in the recreational concourse a few decks down from Operations. The concourses were central atriums populated with shops, entertainment venues, and eateries. This was his domain, among the shopkeepers, and hers was up in the command tower. She berated herself silently for losing touch with their common roots. They had befriended each other as small children, playing in this concourse, under these trees, chasing the nanobot bees. A bond forged in a childhood that felt like it was a lifetime ago.

Lena blinked, momentarily confused when the hung lights in the tree twinkled to life, casting a honeyed glow on Vince's brown face. The artificial daylight had dimmed noticeably, simulating the onset of evening. All the Vega ships still maintained a twenty-four-hour, Earth-like time cycle, and she could have sworn that when she'd bumped into her friend, it had been mid-afternoon.

"Hey, how long have we been chatting?" She glanced around, noticing others checking the time on their devices before resuming their conversations. No one else seemed to have felt the sudden and swift change as acutely.

"Feels like hours." Vince shrugged and tapped the screen of his device. "Oh no! I'm late for my mom's birthday dinner. Why didn't you tell me it was after seven? Christ." He winked at her; his good humor restored. He seamlessly pocketed his own fine from the meter-high etiquette bot that whizzed towards him to issue the blue slip. It buzzed off again without anyone really registering its presence.

Lena's confusion grew but with Vince already turning to leave, she stalled the question on her lips, not wanting him to keep his mom waiting any longer for her favorite son.

"Catch up soon, Lena."

"I'll speak to you tomorrow, Vince. Tell your mom I said, Happy Birthday."

He waved as he set off across the concourse.

Lena frowned, watching him go. Something was up, but she was having trouble pinpointing the cause of her confusion and worry. Her mind refused to believe the reality of the moment, lagging as if she'd been dragged from time and was catching up in fits and starts. The sensation was unsettling, and she glanced around again, trying to make sense of her surroundings. No one else was alarmed, and people were carrying on as if they had not noticed an alteration in the passage of time.

"Odd," she mumbled, resuming her walk back

to her quarters; a journey she swore had only been interrupted for the briefest of visits with her oldest friend, but now appeared to have taken several hours from her already compressed day. Was it possible that she was just overtired? Or perhaps she was coming down with an ailment. Either way, neither thought fully settled her mind around what she was experiencing.

TWO

Alone

Lena woke, her pulse pounding in her ears. The nightmare had been vivid. Being chased was one of her greatest fears. She was glad the surreal experience was only a dream. As a child, she'd hated playing Snag because of the crippling dread at the thought of being pursued. The goal of the game was to reach "safe haven" without being caught by the opposing team's players, but to this day, Lena had never achieved that level. Even as an adult, her anxiety prevented her from fully immersing herself in the fun.

Growing up and living on the *Vega Two* was like growing up in a vacuum. Little had changed in the decades since the ship had launched. The massive generation vessel, along with its sister ships, flew through deep space in search of a new home world.

At last count, the population of passengers and crew aboard stood at just over twenty-eight thousand. Inter-racial, inter-denominational faith groups, inter-disciplinary sciences, and so on. The ships limited population meant that, over time, the mixed contrasts were becoming more of a blended sameness. A sameness she found singularly uninspiring.

"Twenty-eight thousand, three hundred, sixty-two beige and boring souls," Lena murmured, stretching her tan arms over her head and standing up from her small desk in her equally tiny quarters. She craved some excitement, a vivid life with contrast and differences you could recognize and celebrate. Everyone's similarity meant there wasn't much to pique curiosity in the dating pool or stimulate a thought-provoking topic of conversation based on a difference of opinion. It was all so very dull. Right down to their uninspired living quarters.

She lived in a modest cabin located on one of the two decks for single crew members. All accommodations in the singles zone were modest. There wasn't much room for furniture or personal adornments. Crew members were encouraged to focus on their studies and work, which meant maintaining a disciplined lifestyle that didn't leave much room for social activities. There was a saying among the crew that helped make light of the austerity in their lives during training: "Single or mingle. Not both." Luckily, she only had six more months as a bridge crew trainee, then she could upgrade to officers' quarters on the deck above hers where she wasn't aware of any special slogans, but where it was rumored that the parties were wild. That's where she wanted to be. Where living held meaning beyond one's career.

Lena had moved into The Singles, as they called this section of crew quarters, about two years ago. She had kept some reminders of "home" (her family cabin in the general passenger residential quarters) on the three decks below the recreational complex. There was the lamp on her desk that her father had given her when she started her final year of prep at the learning academy. Her most prized possessions were her books. Her mother had gifted her almost all of them, and as paper books were a rare item, they held deep significance for Lena. The bookshelf above her desk held three graphic novels, two science fiction novels, four girl-detective stories, and a book of poetry. The volumes were bookended by two virtual photo frames cycling through images of her family. Her mother and father worked in the recreational concourse (her dad was the manager at the cinema and her mom ran the library and bookstore). They spent most of their lives in the large passenger zones of the ship.

Lena, a newly minted lieutenant, had made her parents proud. She smiled at the photo of her mom and dad on either side of her when she'd been given her officer stripes. She had also been proud of herself that day. All the hard work during training to get her to where she was today, and she still found it tough getting to grips with steering the *Vega Two* through the vast nothingness that surrounded them. Not only did she have a dozen checklists to help her maintain course, but she also had to contend with the captain's efficiency standards and rigorous crew protocols. All this combined to keep comms officers, navigators, engineering, and pilots on their toes during their eight-hour shifts. Her first experience at the helm had been an endless and desperate fight to stay abreast of orders and information requests, reporting and operational duty expectations. Her initial idea that she'd be sitting in a seat, staring into the blackness of space, bored out of her skull, was immediately dispensed with.

She stretched again, feeling her body protest. It had been months since she'd woken to feel anything other than tired. Her self-reflection drifted to thoughts about the demanding workload and routine, and she realized that for the first time in a long time, she felt like she was in front of things. The bridge training rotations were hard but rewarding work. She was relieved she had arrived at an affirmation that her career choices were at least sound.

"Now, if only I could get somewhere with my personal life." A twinge of self-pity assailed her. She'd not dated anyone seriously since starting at the academy, and she was like every other single on the *Vega Two*, anxious about the shallow dating pool. "Not something I can do anything about right now. Work first. Play later, Lena."

She changed, preparing herself for her workday. Mentally, she was ready. Physically, she battled the ache in her neck from falling asleep over her study notes. She still had exams to pass to become a full-time member of the bridge crew. If she ever wanted to fly with the captain, and not just the second-shift commander, she would have to pass a series of demanding tests and get two more promotions.

Captain Mallory ran a tight ship. The *Vega Two* was reputed to have the most disciplined, well-trained crew in the fleet. He prided himself on maintaining that reputation. His captaincy was not only a badge of duty, but one of honor. Lena could only hope she met the man's exacting standards and got to work alongside him one day.

With one last glance in the mirror to make sure she was neat and presentable, she smoothed a hand over her short crew cut, trying to tidy a few stray strands that stubbornly refused to lie flat. She grimaced, tugged her tunic over her hips, and stepped out onto the narrow gangway outside her quarters.

Her footsteps echoed along the strangely quiet deck as she made for the steep stairwell that would take her out of her section.

When she exited the habitation zone and strode across the rec concourse, she was alone. Not another soul traversed the vast space usually bustling with people either working or taking advantage of the numerous retail, entertainment and dining facilities. Lena slowed, glancing around her, uneasy confusion making her pulse quicken.

"Weird . . ."

An etiquette bot rolled past, reduced speed, then carried on after scanning her. Besides the bots cleaning, patrolling, and pruning the large potted trees and shrubs, there was no activity.

Nothing.

She stopped, listening for signs of life. Maybe

everyone was in a gathering she didn't know about. Lifting her device out of her hip pocket, she glanced around again, then tapped the icon for the day's crew schedules. A chill tingled down her spine. She scrolled through the times and activities listed for the day.

"So weird," she repeated. There was nothing scheduled that would cause the busiest part of the *Vega Two* to be completely deserted at eight a.m.

The silence was making her skin crawl, amplifying the inexplicable discomfort which had crept over her the moment she'd entered the concourse. A noise caught her attention and she chastised herself for letting her imagination run wild. She smiled and turned to greet whoever was clattering away near the entrance to a coffee shop, only to find the roll doors gliding up automatically. Then another pair of doors rolled up on a shop across the way.

"Opening time, and yet . . ."

She scanned the various venues around the concourse, concentrating on the dim interiors. Perhaps people were just slow to get moving this morning. The shops opened all around her. After a minute, the clatter of the moving doors died away, replaced by silence. Lights flickered on, but still, no one appeared. Tables and chairs remained stacked, unattended, and the bakery shelves were bare, as were the coffee-shop counters.

"What the actual hell is going on?"

An etiquette bot pivoted, glided towards her and stopped. A moment later, it regurgitated a blue slip of paper from the opening near the top of the domed machine. Lena shook her head and took her fine. She regretted the use of unacceptable language, priding herself on her tight discipline. The bots were shiny and ubiquitous. They were supposed to rein in the behavior of the inhabitants of *Vega Two*. Most of the time, it worked, although the system had been refined many times. The etiquette protocols prevented major disruptions, and even though there were those (like her friend Vince) who bent the rules sometimes, the ship was a peaceful and safe vessel. Captain Mallory wouldn't have it any other way.

"Maybe, this once, the cap will understand. I mean, this place is a ghost town, and I am a little freaked out right now," she muttered, ill at ease with her monologue, but unable to stem the need to fill the silence with speech. She walked on, a cold dread clutching at her from every dim shop interior, and every dark corner of the echoing emptiness surrounding her. Lena hastened her steps, her solo footfall the only sound in the emptiness. The echo of her steps soon fell away into an eerie hush when she left the large, open space for the confines of narrow corridors.

The walkways, elevators, and galleries of the ship's operational zone were equally deserted. Lena tried to breathe normally, panic her only companion. Her pulse pounded, and she searched her thoughts for possible explanations, coming up blank with each passing moment. Had she missed some vital communique about a ship-wide evacuation, or something? Where the hell was everyone? What could be happening that had apparently left her the sole occupant of the *Vega Two?*

The elevator door slid open, signaling her arrival at the bridge. She stepped out and was greeted by yet another space devoid of people. She had honestly expected the bridge to be crewed and busy. The questions poised on the tip of her tongue for the duty officer changed to a sucked in breath-turned-hiccup. Her panic was rising.

"Hello?" Lena looked around, unsure. What should she do if she was the only one on the bridge? "Ah, jeez. I don't know if I need to wait, or go, or . . . or . . ."

She sighed heavily, lifting her hands in an exasperated gesture. Her fingers trembled, and she squeezed her hand into a fist. Uncertainty and indecision made it hard to make sense of this bizarre experience.

She walked to her station, looking around one more time, willing another person to appear, then sat down to activate the helm's control panels. The glass and metal were cool to the touch, the seat squeaked, and she scanned the bridge, observing the blink of lights, the odor of cleaning agent and the click and hum of electronics. She turned and blinked at the display, reached out, and ran her hand over the buttons and sliders. They responded to her biometrics, glowing and ready.

This wasn't a dream. It didn't feel like a dream. There was a sense of wakefulness, of reality, and yet, this whole morning felt like the most unreal thing she could remember experiencing. Lena's uncertainty and doubt threatened to overwhelm her. A quick hysterical laugh bubbled before she clamped her lips closed. She slouched back in her chair, a flash of embarrassed guilt searing her mind. The captain would not approve of her loss of composure.

"But the captain's not here. No one is." As factual as her statement was, it only served to remind her that the situation was highly unusual. Her mind reeled and she bounced back to denial, unable to mentally process the magnitude of her dilemma.

Maybe I just need to wait for someone to show up, she thought. An almost instant intuition told her that was unlikely to happen.

She drummed her fingers on the console in front of her, desperate to figure out what to do next. An idea occurred to her, and she reached for her device again.

"Call Mom."

The device signaled its attempt to connect her call. There was no answer. The screen refreshed, asking her to leave a message. She tapped the record button and said, "Hi, Mom. Are you there? Hello?" She waited only a second, then cleared her throat. If her loneliness had been uncomfortable before, it became acutely painful in that moment. "Okay, well . . . I just wanted to check in with you and see if you're okay. There's something weird happening today. I don't know if you've noticed, but there's no one else around on the main levels . . . okay, call me back when you can."

She clicked the call end icon and tossed the device onto the console, her breath catching on a whimper. This was very definitely a loss of composure, and she thought, *Oh, screw it! I think that under the circumstances, the captain might understand.*

Her throat hurt and she swallowed against unshed

tears. Waves of shivers made her teeth chatter. Her thoughts descended into the dark possibility of being left behind. Alone. How could that have happened?

"No," she shook her head, swiping at a tear on her cheek, "it's not possible! Something else is going on, and I need to figure it out." Shaking her head again, her lips pursed and her spine straight, Lena got to work. She knew she wasn't supposed to be on the bridge unsupervised, but she also didn't want to leave in case the rest of the crew finally showed up for their shift.

"Wait, there was no outgoing crew, either." None of the other stations were active. She turned back to hers and checked the activity log. The last pilot had signed on for shift at midnight, but they had not signed off. The station had been idle for over four hours, approximately halfway into third shift.

She moved to the navigator's station and checked the activity log there. It, too, had last been active four hours ago.

"So, whatever's going on has a defined start point. Okay. That's more than I knew when this crazy day began. Progress is progress, right?"

She confirmed that all the other stations displayed the same activity log results. Something had happened while she was asleep and she had a time stamp for it, at least.

Lena went back to her console and called up the course display. "Flight computer check." The computer chimed, listening for her voice command. "Check course activity for 0400 hours."

"Vega Two on course until zero four ten. Course deviation detected at zero four eleven. Course correction not completed."

"Shit, a course deviation? How?"

An etiquette panel near her issued a blue fine. She ignored it.

"Unknown. Please specify query."

"Computer, show on-screen the course deviation and plot current and future course using available data from deviation." She had to focus on giving the voice commands succinctly. Her mind was a sea of questions and her anxiety grew with each new development. A course deviation was bad news.

If the Vega Two was off course by even a few degrees, they would miss their destination by millions of kilometers. The Vega mission was launched from the near-Earth base at the second Le Grange point about eighty years before Lena was born. Generations of people lived, worked and passed aboard the ships designed as humanity's last hope of continuity. With

Earth a devastated wasteland, the only option was to trek across the universe to the closest, most viable alternative to the planet that had been the origin of their species.

One such planet, Vega X45-1, was the target for the mission's ships, more than twenty in total. The arc-sized vessels were designed to transport a collection of species, both plants and animals alike, and their human saviors. But that planet was several hundred years away in the distant Vega star system. Life would have to continue on the ships, and in order to do that, they had to be massive. As big as the ships were, they were still a tiny speck in comparison to the Cosmos they sailed through.

A fractional change in the course of their vessel could signal complete disaster for the ship and its passengers, knocking them off the exact trajectory they needed to stay on to even come close to the far-off land they sought. The course change that had happened at zero four eleven was big. A few degrees off mark. Not only that, Lena discovered that the Vega Two was also accelerating.

"No, no, no. This is not good."

She checked the engineering logs. There was no discernible change in power output, only the minimum of which was needed to keep the ship clipping along at its staggering speed, small retrorockets making tiny corrections from time to time. No command had been given to speed up. So, why was the ship accelerating? And why was it doing it on a course taking them away from their route?

"Calculate and plot a new trajectory, factoring in current course deviation and acceleration."

"Calculating. This may take several minutes."

THREE

The Twins

"Captain to the bridge. Priority one." Lena took her finger off the navigation console's communication button, losing hope with every passing moment. She sat back, closed her eyes, and concentrated on her breathing. When she felt calmer, she blinked, mentally setting aside the anxiety that threatened to send her into a tailspin again.

Her call went unanswered. No one arrived. Twenty minutes after her shift began, she was still the sole officer on the bridge. Neither the captain, nor her mother, had responded. The computer remained silent, busy calculating the *Vega Two's* new trajectory.

Lena stared at her reflection in the smoky glass of the dormant controls. Wild thoughts of the whole thing being some sadistic, practical joke were gone. Vince would never have been able to mastermind such a widespread scheme. At least, she didn't think he was behind this. She would definitely spend the night in the brig for what she planned to do to him if it turned out he was responsible for making her the butt of such a cruel prank. Again, she dismissed the idea. There was just no way the rest of the crew would cooperate on such a scale to play a joke on a junior officer.

She sat down at the Nav's station, using activity to keep calm. It didn't help being in a state of mind-numbing panic. It made it impossible to focus on anything other than how desperate she was for answers. Her smooth reflection belied her inner turmoil. She spent a futile hour trying to assess the true nature of her problems and formulate a plan.

What she needed was to gain access to the navigation controls. Nothing she had tried so far had worked. She was locked out by command-level codes. As a trainee officer, her rank was insufficient for what she wanted to do. A commander was supposed to authorize any system changes.

"And as we have already established, there are no goddamn commanders around!" She yelled, slapping her hand on her armrest, the chair pivoting away from the workstation.

The fines from the etiquette console were now a

ribbon of blue paper snaking towards the floor a few paces from her chair. She was going in the brig when all of this was over, that much was a guarantee. She scowled at the machine with its long blue tongue. Why was *that* the only system she seemed to be able to influence? It was more than frustrating that she was essentially locked out of the controls because she lacked the rank to execute the commands. She made a note to speak to her supervisor about greater redundancy measures for future interruptions in staffing, all the while forcing herself to ignore the tidal wave of thoughts that suggested there would be no future meetings with her S.O., or anyone else for that matter.

Stomping back to her chair at the helm, she sank into it and spun to stare at the main screen again.

"Somehow, I'm going to have to find a way into those systems. Think, Lena. What do you need?"

Her mind was blank, and she growled, angry and upset at her apparent incompetence. She rose and paced the bridge, calling up status reports for each section and operational area of the *Vega Two*. She stopped suddenly when a troublesome thought occurred to her: why had she not also disappeared, along with everyone else? All the life pods were still on board. No one had *left* the ship. They had simply *vanished*. So why hadn't she? She was the only one around. What difference would it make if she changed the ship's course or not?

That question was followed by a flood of anxiety. It was getting difficult to hold the crippling feeling at bay and her stress caused her knotted, tense neck muscles to ache. The isolation and lack of progress with the trajectory calculations made the passage of time feel like days, not hours.

What if the deviation in course was connected to the disappearance of the crew? What if correcting the ship's course could, by some small chance, fix everything else?

"Don't give up. Think, Lena. What do you need?"

She checked again on the status of the computer's calculation. Time remaining five minutes. Why was it taking so long?

"Argh!"

Her hands flew over the panel in front of her. The science officer's station was big, with many additional controls. She felt like a trespasser but persisted, determined to do anything and everything in her power to return the situation to normal as soon as possible. She instructed the ship's sensors to do a series of sweeps, recalling the anomalous readings Wu had told Commander Morris about during Lena's last shift.

"Sensors detect no harmful emissions," the computer responded, the voice a flat, AI-generated monotone.

Lena keyed in another command and hit Enter.

"Sensors detect no hull breaches or other damage. Structural integrity nominal."

Lena huffed. "What else . . . Let's see . . ." Her fingers typed, slid through glowing options in front of her, then punched the Enter command again.

"Sensors detect no life support changes. Systems are nominal."

"Shit." The ribbon of blue paper sagged to the floor. She stuck her tongue out at the fines, determined to get the better of that machine when she had a chance.

"Ship wide hail from the bridge, this is Lieutenant Dixon. If you hear this, please respond."

Silence. She entered a new sensor sweep command.

"Sensors show one life sign aboard."

Yeah. Mine.

"This cannot be real. This has to be a dream. Jesus." The etiquette wall panel flashed at her. A bot showed up, flashing red lights and making strident demands.

"Report to Security immediately," it said in a thin, tinny voice.

"Fuck off." She hit the reset panel at the back of the

machine and rolled it off the bridge into a side corridor. When the doors closed behind her, she opened the manual override panel and locked down the bridge. She didn't have the executive overrides for the bots, but at least she had the ability to turn off individual units and to keep them from bothering her until she'd figured out what was going on. She had attended a security briefing last month to discuss the potential shortcomings of the etiquette bots and Lena didn't want to take chances with bots that could turn into aggressors.

A disaster on another Vega ship had meant all the bots on the *Vega Two* were retrofitted with a self-isolating controller and a manual reset panel. The etiquette software had also been updated to include a few back doors to prevent a lockout by the system. The other ship's AI had taken control of the computer systems, killed some people, and used the bots to almost kill the captain of that ship. No such incident could happen once the retrofit recommendations were in place on the other vessels in the fleet.

The fleet.

Of course! She could hail the other ships in the Vega fleet. There had to be one within range of the deep-space communication beacons. At least, that was her hope. The comms beacons were self-propelled communication satellites linking the entire fleet to each other in a vast array. They had been sent out to light the path for the Vega mission, launching a decade earlier than the mission's flagship, the *Vega One.* That expansive network of beacons could help her establish a link to the closest ship to request assistance. The question remained, though, would they answer?

Lena sat down at the communications console and waved her hand over the dark controls. When they came to life, she activated the keyboard. She typed a quick message.

Vega Two general distress call. Crew and passengers, all missing. No explanation at this time. One soul remaining on board. Please send help.

She added the ship's coordinates and the trajectory information she had available. The computer was still processing the new course deviation, so the old data would have to do. With a deep breath, and more hope than she had dared to feel all morning, Lena sent the message, praying there was at least one ship within a few weeks travel of the *Vega Two.* As only the second vessel to launch from the fleet, she understood they were years ahead of many of the later ships. Her only hope was the *Vega Three.* The fleet had lost contact with *Vega One* only eight years into its long journey. She had not been heard from again. Her loss was memorialized every year on August eighth with a solemn ceremony and the ejection of a wreath into space. Lena usually went to the celebration of life party afterwards feeling guilty for the loss of an entire ship, but also feeling disconnected from the tragedy that had happened decades before she was even born.

"Please, God, let the *Vega Three* be close enough to respond to my message." She muttered, clinging to the tiny sliver of hope the message ignited in the darkness of her desperation. This morning had worn her out and she was tired, frustrated and scared. She had no idea what to do about the missing crew and passengers. "I don't want us to end up being another tragic story for the Vega children to study in history lessons."

"Course trajectory calculated."

"Ah, finally, thank you." Was it odd to thank the computer? She shrugged and sat down at the helm console again and called up the new trajectory. Lena's alarm spiked. The ship was already far off course. Without intervention, the deviation would only worsen.

She hadn't really paid attention to the passing hours, and it was a surprise to see the amount of time that had passed since she'd first asked for the calculation. It should not have taken the computer almost her entire shift to make the trajectory calculation.

"Computer, add supplemental note for navigation control. Note is as follows. Run general functionality diagnostic of—" She stopped, struck by the futility of the instruction.

"Incomplete instruction. Please repeat," the soulless voice prompted as she stared at the screen. The silence around her became a deafening rush, emphasizing the acute loneliness Lena had been attempting to hold at bay for hours. She imagined the crew, busy and working at their stations, the conversations, the sense of other people surrounding her.

"Disregard," she muttered in a low, shaky voice. For a moment, she indulged in a wave of self-pity, swallowing hard against the onslaught of emotions that threatened to undo her self-control. She sniffed, wiped her nose with the back of her hand, and shook her head. "Okay. That's enough of that. What would the captain say if he saw you sniveling on the bridge?"

Her shift was almost over, and yet her internal clock told her the timing felt off. Instead of focusing on the sensed disparity, she rationalized the odd feeling as a condition of her ordeal.

"Right, back to it. Where was I?" She blinked and sat up straight, her mind back on task. "Let's try sensor sweeps along the new trajectory. Computer, enhance sector grid 3B," she said, squinting at the screen. The large, dark sector lay dead ahead, whereas yesterday it had been at eighteen degrees to starboard bow. She remembered it was the area of space they had been gathering data on during her previous shift and she wanted to see more clearly what they were moving towards.

"Enhancing."

The screen blanked then rendered a higher definition picture of the space ahead of the ship. "Computer, what is that region of space composed of?"

"Unknown."

"Well, that can't be good." She squinted again. "Computer, can you enhance the visual again?"

"Enhancing."

The image rendered and Lena stepped back to take in the full picture.

"It can't be. Computer, do a sensor sweep for gravitational waves."

"Gravitational waves detected in sector 3B."

"Create a visual representation over the on-screen image using far-infrared, and X-Ray, please."

The image changed. White glowing lines flowed around a duo of dark spots, tightening and bunching at the edges of the spots and in the narrow space between them.

"Oh, God." She swallowed hard and said in a strangled voice, "Computer, calculate approximate time to intercept."

"Calculating."

Lena stared at the rendering, icy terror pulsing through her.

"Intercept will occur in three days, sixteen hours."

She plopped into a seat. It was useless knowing this information, of course. It meant little. The accretion disks of the twin black holes visible through the visualization on-screen were already disrupting the normal passage of time. The display clock showed her shift had ended, and yet her internal time had her believing it was only a handful of hours since she first arrived on the bridge.

Black holes played havoc with time, dilating, overlapping and compressing it in mercurial ways. Was this anomaly also responsible for the disappearance of everyone else on the *Vega Two?*

So many puzzles, and she was on an unpredictable schedule, attempting to solve them. The challenge seemed insurmountable.

"Computer, is there an emergency override to

correct the ship's course?"

"Command codes are required to alter course. You are not authorized to alter the ship's course."

"Can't blame a girl for trying, I suppose." The computer wasn't equipped to know how to circumvent the command chain, and neither was Lena when she thought about it. If only she had those codes.

"Computer, are there hard copies of the codes in a manual or some other repository?"

"Affirmative." She waited, but there were no elaborations as to where the hard copies were.

"Think, Lena . . ." She swung around on the swivel chair she had been slouching in, scanning the bridge with fresh eyes. "Where would something like that be kept?"

Nothing jumped out at her and she slumped back, feeling immensely sorry for herself and wishing she was still asleep at her desk. What could soothe her nerves? How could she clear her mind of the panic that threatened her ability to function?

FOUR

Who's there?

The vodka sloshed onto the counter, pooling next to her shot glass. "Whoops!" Lena giggled and tried again, successfully topping off the glass on her second attempt.

She perched at the officers' bar, staring out across the deserted concourse.

"Cheers!"

With a flick of her wrist, she threw back the drink, coughing from the fiery kick of the alcohol, then wiped her mouth on her sleeve and tossed the glass onto the bar.

Sliding off the stool, she steadied herself for a moment, her head swimming. She wasn't a heavy drinker, so the liquor went to work quickly. The vodka took the edge off the tension that had been ratcheting up since she'd gained a partial understanding of what was going on aboard the *Vega Two*. With her situation dire, and after exhausting all the logical options to solve her problem, Lena decided a little brain lubrication wouldn't hurt to loosen the cogs of imagination. At the same time, the vodka helped her relax. It was a necessary tonic considering her perilous mental state.

She tapped the side of her head as she slouched against a large tree pot for a moment. "Time to get the ol' brain into a different mode, but first, I gotta pee." She snorted and giggled as an etiquette bot approached.

Before it even had a chance to issue new fines, she flipped the reset switch and shoved it in a maintenance closet. Yanking the manual override handle for the door, she cranked it left, locking the offending bot inside, then staggered away in the direction of the nearest bathrooms.

A mild terror had perched on her shoulder until the first shot of vodka warmed her belly. After that, she hadn't cared quite as much. The place didn't feel as lonely as it had when she had left the bridge. The deserted concourse, usually full of activity after her shifts, seemed less threatening through the haze of alcohol.

Lena took a left turn and walked down a tiled

passage, entering the mall's public bathrooms. Water dripped into a metal basin, and it was easy to imagine that the quiet and empty space had very recently been shared by another occupant.

"Hello?" She waited only a moment. "Of course, the toilets are void of life, just like everywhere else around here," she said, her words slurring a little. The stall door banged when she came out, and it echoed as much through her booze-soaked brain as it did in the tiled bathroom. She stared at her face in the mirror and washed her hands. Without warning, a second reflection appeared a short distance to her left. A quick glance confirmed what she knew—there was no one else there.

"Seeing double already? Good thing I stopped at three shots of vodka."

But something took hold in the far reaches of her mind, pushing back the drink haze fogging her thoughts. It had felt, for a split second, as if there had been someone else in the bathroom with her.

"Shit. Stop it, Lena." She slapped her hands on the basin, then sidled over to the hand dryer. Unnerved by her train of thought, she refused to look at the mirrors in the bathroom again. The terror of being alone had morphed into something far more sinister, her imagination taking hold of a ghoulish hallucination.

She emerged from the bathroom, a shiver shooting down her spine. Goosebumps puckered the flesh on her arms.

"So typical of you to let your imagination run wild like that. Get it together and focus on what's in front of you." Her head swam, the alcohol causing her thoughts tumble over each other.

Weaving back through the concourse, she watched the shutters come down on the quiet shops, locking up for the night. The jarring fast-forward surprised her again. This time, it was accompanied by an unnerving knowledge of what caused the erratic changes.

Black holes. Not one, but *two*.

The doors clattered against the cool floor tiles, the chorus of activity fading into a deathly stillness accompanied by the change in the park-like atrium's ambient lighting. If it was at all possible, the shutting of the empty mall was even more eerie than when she'd watched the doors rise on the empty shops at the beginning of her day.

"All locked up. Safe and sound," she murmured, attempting to normalize what she had just witnessed.

The last words passing her lips, *safe and sound,* caused a cascade of memories, the edges of an idea coalescing in her inebriated mind.

"Argh, focus!" she cursed, then scrunched her eyes closed to help lasso the errant thoughts. Slowing to a stop, she swayed slightly in the middle of the empty concourse, tapping her chin. Then, with a quick shrug, she set off again. "Any old plan is worth a try at this point." Her speech sounded odd, muffled and distorted. She sagged against a wall to recover her balance.

The alcohol was taking hold of her faster, and with more dramatic effect than she'd anticipated. After a few deep breaths, Lena continued weaving her way up through the residential zone until she reached the deck that housed the senior officers, stopping every so often to let her dizziness abate so she could orient herself.

The decks she was traversing were unfamiliar territory. She had rarely been in this part of the ship before. The corridors were wide, the stairs not as steep as in the lower decks. A stray thought about how she might, one day, live in the senior officers' deck quarters made her smile and lose her concentration.

She stumbled up the last step, barely recovering her stride when a quick movement flashed in the corner of her eye from the balcony above.

She paused, staring. Had she imagined it or was the alcohol playing tricks on her mind, shifting static items in her vision as she steadily descended into a state of fall-down drunkenness? How had three shots of vodka turned her brain so completely to mush?

The answer came a moment later when her stomach growled.

"That was probably a mistake." A mild queasiness confirmed what she already knew. Besides the liquor, her stomach was empty, and about to rebel on her.

She climbed the stairs, her attention fixed on the treads beneath her feet, the ground swaying in a sickening undulating beat that matched the pulse throbbing in her temple.

A sound like the hush of a fan, and the briefest glimpse of a human form at the top of the stairs caught her off guard and she grabbed for the railing, sliding to the floor. She held onto the railing, righting herself, daring only a quick glance up at the empty landing.

"Hello?" Her head pounded a painful rhythm in response to her raised voice. Lena squeezed her eyes shut for a moment when she reached the top step. Of course, there was no greeting in answer. What had she expected?

She turned, looking back down into the darkened concourse. Even the small birds that usually flitted about were absent. Had she just seen a bird? Her brow creased, deepening when she recalled the face in the mirror in the bathroom.

That was not a bird, Lena.

A wave of nausea made her stop and suck in a deep breath. A primal fear coursed through her. Her pulse throbbed in the back of her mouth. The old terror of being chased soaked into every part of her consciousness and her breathing faltered, coming in ragged gasps that only exacerbated the nausea overtaking her. She hated the game, Snag, and the dread it always induced when she was dragged into it by Vince or other friends.

But this was not a game of Snag. It was the same fear, but a different cause, a far less benign cause than a childhood game.

"Holy Fuck."

Icy alarm froze her to the spot for what seemed like an eternity. She was too scared to do anything but cling to the cool, metal railing at the top of the stairs and try not to heave up the contents of her now churning belly.

With great effort, she forced herself to think. She slowed her breathing and waited for her fright to recede to a manageable level. Her mind was filled with a combination of soothing memories of her mother cuddling with her as a child, overlayed by a stern monologue that explained in clipped tones that it was entirely possible her stress and persistent panic were playing tricks on her, that she had nothing to fear and that she was, in fact, quite safe.

It didn't work. The more she tried to convince herself that she was alone, and what she'd experienced was a figment of her overtired, overwrought brain, the louder her senses screamed that she had not imagined it all. She felt a tangible presence. What was it?

Lena's eyes grew wide, a shiver passing down her arms and neck, her teeth beginning a loud clattering in her jaw.

She sensed *something* there. With her.

In a moment of blinding clarity, Lena knew she was not alone anymore, and her knees turned to jelly. In the same instant, she also knew it couldn't be another person. No. There was an incorporeal nature to what she'd experienced so far; there, but not there. Only one possibility remained, and she didn't want to articulate the thought for fear of manifesting something horrific.

Another movement across the landing caught her eye. Her rapid pulse was accompanied by a loud rushing of blood in her ears. Her mouth was dry, and her throat constricted. She waited, wishing she was anywhere else but where she was, in that moment, confronting what could only be described as her worst nightmare. Lena was being chased, or followed; spied on at the very least, by something that didn't belong on the ship. Not a single coherent thought formed in her panic-soaked mind.

It took a monumental effort to shift from where she still clung to the stairs railing. She desperately sought the safety of shelter, the exposed position at the top of the stairs indefensible. If she could just get to that small alcove down the corridor.

Focusing on putting one foot in front of the other to reach the security of her destination, Lena's determination grew. Without warning, reality itself seemed to shift, a shadow danced on the wall at the meeting of two passages near her intended hiding spot. She froze again, staring, unable to look away from that cool shade, expecting monsters and praying for angels.

"Please stop this!" Her voice trembled, bouncing off the panels of the deck's corridor with its closed doors and silent walls. "If someone is there, just come out. We can talk. I won't hurt you."

Adrenaline on top of the vodka made her lightheaded, and she blinked, shivered, and slumped against the wall, breathing hard. She desperately wished now that she'd stayed locked in the safety of the bridge.

After several moments of crippling anticipation,

she summoned the will to creep forward. Her instincts screamed at her to run in the opposite direction. She was pleased and relieved to discover the thought of fleeing seemed irrational, which meant she was thinking again. She had been taught that you can't solve problems with your feelings. Her training surged now, and she squared her shoulders, feeling a little braver and calmer.

Her father's mantra came to her. *One step at a time. One problem at a time. Keep moving forward.*

She wasn't alone anymore, and that was a good thing, right?

She reached the end of the corridor and peered around the corner, almost too afraid to look. She fought her trepidation and stepped into the middle of the next long passage at the exact same moment as a shadow formed against the wall not twenty paces from her.

Lena felt the warmth drain from her face. What she saw there, without it really being there, was unbelievable.

"Sweet Jesus, what is that?" she whispered, her knees shaking.

The apparition steadied, holding her gaze in its gleaming stare. She could see right through it, to the wall behind, which seemed impossible. It was hard to get a mental grasp on the vision. Her mind refused to accept what she saw as real. A trickle of sweat ran down her back. The shadowy figure moved, imperceptibly at first, then advanced on her in the blink of an eye. Lena shrieked and threw her arms over her head, cowering.

A cool breeze swept past her, and she quaked from head to toe, fear sobering her instantly. She spun and emptied the contents of her stomach right there in the middle of the corridor of the senior officers' quarters.

Confused and more scared than she could ever remember being, she stayed doubled over until her body stopped convulsing. With her focus entirely on retching up the alcohol, she had failed to pay attention to the wraith-like apparition and where it had gone.

Through the tears that had formed in her eyes from the effort of purging the contents of her stomach, she checked first left, then right. She was alone. The apparition was gone. Lena sensed nothing but the quiet emptiness of the ship again. She shifted to a bench and sank onto it to cradle her aching head in her hands.

It took a full five minutes for her to process what had just happened. A shaky breath hitched on a sob, and she covered her face with her hands, crying. Today was testing her on so many levels.

Why was this happening? What could it all mean? She knew that if she didn't find a way to alter the *Vega*

Two's course, and soon, she would die.

"And now it seems my final hours will be haunted, too. It's so unfair!"

She didn't believe in ghosts. Her mother was the religious one. Lena had found it difficult to follow her mother's faith practices and, at the age of fourteen, declared she would no longer attend chapel. Science left little room for faith, especially in the far reaches of space, surrounded by a great nothingness that made it clear they were very much alone in the universe.

"Well, alone with twenty-eight thousand other people until this morning. That's, technically, not alone. This—me by myself for the past few fucking hours—this is alone. Jesus."

An etiquette bot rolled up, and she flipped its switch. "I'm running out of places to stow you little bastards." She looked at it and sighed. As irritating as they were, they came straight to her when she used colorful language. In a way, it was comforting. "It would be funny if it weren't so annoying." She rose and put her hand on the dome of the bot. With a hard shove, she pushed it over and shrugged. That would work.

"You can't get up if I knock you over. Seems pretty simple to me." She walked away, resuming her previous mission to infiltrate the captain's cabin and retrieve his computer codes.

When she arrived at the closed doors, she found the manual override panel and followed the procedure to open the doors by hand. It took a few tries, but when she heard the locks slide back, she knew she'd succeeded.

She pressed her fingers into the thin crease between the panels and tried to pry them apart. A small gap opened, and she grunted with satisfaction, adjusting her stance. The doors were heavier than they appeared, and she fiddled and worked her fingers into the space she'd made between them until she had a good hold on the panels. She tugged at them again with all her might.

A cool breeze greeted her, and she glanced up and straight into the wizened face of the apparition that had spooked her in the corridor earlier.

"Mother of God!"

Lena tumbled back from the door, landing on her butt. She scrambled away, but the ghostly visitor stayed just inside the entrance to the captain's quarters, content to stare at her for a moment. Lena's heart pounded, her hands shook, and she could barely catch her breath, unable to look away.

FIVE

The Captain's Codes

Losing some of her fear when the apparition remained just beyond the open doors, Lena stared. Her mind raced and she couldn't help but take in the details of the otherworldly figure.

Humanoid. Female. A blaze of white, shaggy hair. Old and hunched. The clothing appeared to be some kind of uniform, but it was faded and unrecognizable. Lena squinted, her curiosity slowly replacing her initial shock and horror.

"Are you okay?" The voice was a whisper, like a thought from the back of her mind.

"Holy cow! Did you just talk to me?" She stared at the diaphanous figure who had crossed her arms, waiting.

"I did. It's okay. I won't hurt you."

"Then why the hell did you scare the crap out of

me back there?"

"I find it difficult to control how I appear, or where. I am sorry for scaring you, Lena."

"You know my name? How?"

"Hard to explain right now, but in time, you'll come to understand." The voice echoed quietly, like a resonating hiss stuck in something hollow.

Lena couldn't help the goose flesh that crept over her body as she rose, absently dusting off the seat of her pants. The entire experience was as unnatural as anything she'd ever encountered. Approaching the door with caution, she peered at the ghostly figure, feeling only moderately bolder.

"Who are you? Are you human?"

"I am human. *Who* I am is harder to explain. But we don't have time for all of that now. You have to stop the ship from drifting towards the black holes."

"You know a lot about what's going on. Did you cause this? Have you taken control of our ship? Where is everyone? What did you do with them?" The questions tumbled from her in a cascade of relief at finally having someone else to talk to until she stopped short of the final question which screamed in her mind. She could not ask if they were still alive. The thought of her parents being dead and gone took her breath away.

"Lena, I know what is happening, and I will explain, but right now, let's deal with how to stop it. You have a plan."

"Of course." The reminder of her task—to find the command codes—jarred her from her runaway thoughts. She had developed a throbbing headache and rubbed her temple.

"That hangover is going to hurt for a few days if you don't take something now. The captain has pain meds on his vanity."

Lena shot her ethereal companion a suspicious look, then thought better of commenting on the ghost's apparent prescience. If she'd been followed around all morning, it stood to reason her actions had been observed, including her short visit to the bar.

The apparition gave her a nod, then drifted aside, beckoning her to enter the captain's quarters.

Lena tugged at the doors again, still apprehensive about the hovering apparition.

"How do I know I can trust you not to harm me?"

"I am here to help make things right, get the ship back to the status quo. Even if you don't trust me, you need me."

"Good point." Lena wandered through the cabin, a wash of shame making her uncomfortable when she thought of how mad Captain Mallory would be at the intrusion on his private space. In his bathroom, the vanity shelf was neat and clean. A bottle of pain killers, with a prescription label, revealed another small detail about the man she both revered and feared. His first name was Joe.

"Captain Joe Mallory. Cool." She shook two pain killer tabs into her palm and swallowed them with a swig of water from the faucet.

"Feel better?" The hollow voice rushed at her in the confines of the bright bathroom.

She jumped. Her new companion waited in the doorway, bowed and translucent.

"Jesus. Stop sneaking up on me, for the love of all things good and holy!" Lena knew she sounded harsh, but every time the old woman suddenly appeared, she almost peed her pants. Lena could not suppress her terror completely, and it kept her on edge and vigilant.

"I'm sorry if I scare you. I don't have any way to alleviate your discomfort at my appearance or my presence, but believe me when I say it is essential for me to be here. I suggest we focus on the problem at hand."

"You sound impatient."

"If you knew what I knew, you'd understand. Now,

let's go."

Lena turned to find herself alone in the captain's cabin. Her visitor was nowhere in sight.

"Great. I sense another jump scare coming on. Now I know what Pavlov's dog must have felt like." She was annoyed but couldn't help but feel mild relief that her weird, new companion had some of the answers for the hundreds of questions that had plagued her all morning.

"Seriously though, is a ghost for company much better than the infinite loneliness of space?" She couldn't decide. "Seems we can add a dose of crazy to that shopping list of things you will have to fix today."

Lena shivered, stepping back through the half-open doors of the captain's quarters and out into the quiet passage beyond.

"Hello? Do I still need to get the captain's codes?" *I can't believe I'm talking to a ghost.*

"You do, but they're not in there." The voice came to her in a soft whisper from nearby, and Lena pivoted to see a suggestion of movement a little way down the corridor. She shuddered, growing annoyed with the detached and ethereal voice. It swirled and seemed to travel through her at times, unnerving her.

"Then why did you insist I go into the captain's

room?" she asked after she'd recovered from her fresh scare. *This ghost is going to turn* my *hair gray!*

"Pain killers. For your hangover." The words echoed off the walls.

"Damn. Stop talking like that. It's super creepy."

"Sorry. It can't be helped. Believe it or not, I'm yelling as loud as I can just so you can hear me. Sound passing between your world and mine loses much of its energy."

"Oh. How do you . . .? Wait, I know—no time for those types of questions. Save the ship first."

"Good. I knew you'd adjust quickly to the demands of the current circumstances. You've always been a quick study."

Lena stared at the ghostly woman, struck by a sudden familiarity.

"Mom, is that you?"

A chuckle, sounding more like the tinkling of glass, echoed back at her softly. "I'm not your mother, Lena."

"Oh, thank God!" Her relief was palpable. What could have been a potentially grief-inducing revelation was neutralized.

"For someone who's not religious, you sure are invoking the Lord's name a bunch today."

"Says the ghost I'm talking to." She raised an

eyebrow and came to a stop, crossing her arms, annoyed at the taunt.

"Ah, but that's where you're wrong."

"How so?" she challenged.

"I'm not a ghost."

SIX

The Veil of Space-Time

"Now I'm confused." Lena cocked her head, her brows knitting. The thought that someone was playing some kind of sick joke on her returned and she looked around, her annoyance flaring. Her thoughts turned angry. *Vince, I will make you pay, I swear!*

"I understand, and no, this is not a practical joke. Vince has nothing to do with what is happening here. I don't blame you for having mixed emotions right now, but can we get back to our mission, please?"

Lena followed a trail she sensed more than observed. The apparition was always only in her peripheral vision—the tiniest of movements, the quickest of flashes—leading her forward.

She arrived back at the bridge, still having encountered empty corridors and no obvious signs of the other occupants of the *Vega Two.*

"I already tried everything I could on the bridge. Without the captain's override codes, I'm locked out of critical systems."

"I know." The echoed statement brushed past Lena, and she took a few steps to the left to face the door to the commander's briefing room. She shuddered at the closeness she sensed by her cheek and shook her head to dispel the need to cringe away from the unnatural contact.

"In there?" she asked in a measured voice.

"Yes."

Lena got to work opening the door. It opened with less effort than the captain's quarters had. "At least I've learned something today. I now know how to gain manual access to these doors," she muttered, slipping through a narrow gap and into the briefing room.

An oval table with control panels dominated the space, eight chairs pushed in around it. There was a large display screen at the far end with an etched ship's schematic on the responsive acrylic panel. Lights blinked at intervals, illuminating diagnostics for various systems currently showing on-screen. The schematic would cycle through several of these panels as the automated diagnostics ran in hour-long intervals.

A cold blast pushed past Lena, and she turned to

see her ghostly visitor standing at the head of the table.

"In here." The voice was muffled, and she strained to hear the words.

"Okay." Lena sat down in the captain's chair, running her hand over the smooth glass until she found the circular depression that indicated a compartment. She pushed the release and the compartment rose silently from the surface of the table.

"Second drawer." The whisper was right next to her ear and Lena cringed, unable to prevent the instinctive cower this time. A small chuckle came from the old woman.

"It's not funny."

"You'll be laughing with me when all of this is over."

"Well, that sounds like you're telling me I'm going to die. Thanks for that!" She had been actively suppressing thoughts about her own doom and being reminded that she could soon be dead made her angry.

"You are a hothead jumping straight to that conclusion. Let's just say that if you do what I tell you, you'll live a long and happy life."

Lena took a deep breath and opened the second drawer of the compartment. Inside was a card key. It was the size of her palm, and she swiveled in the chair to look for her companion.

"Come to the bridge."

The apparition disappeared, seemingly evaporating through the bulkhead, as if it wasn't even there.

Lena rounded the table and left the briefing room through the gap in the doors.

An echo danced off the walls of the bridge. "Sit in the captain's chair and slot the key card into his control panel."

Lena followed the instructions and the moment the key card clicked into its slot, the panel lit up. "Shit, it's asking for a verification code." She stared at the small screen, frowning.

"Alpha-Two, Sigma-Six."

She shot the hovering shape a surprised look. "How do you know that?"

"I'll tell you in a moment. Just enter the code."

"Okay. Here goes." Lena typed in the code and watched the screen refresh to show her a running thread of read-outs from all over the ship. "We're in."

Silence.

Glancing around the bridge, she appeared to have lost her companion again. Had the apparition been generated by the computer as a way to assist her with her access to the bridge controls?

It seemed unlikely, but on second thought, nothing she'd experienced so far today had any semblance of reality.

"Okay. Let's see what I can do about the trajectory of the ship." Lena scrolled a list of operational instructions, looking for a way to configure the ship's navigation systems. "Computer, do I have voice access to navigation control?"

"Affirmative."

"Computer, configure a new course trajectory to correct the deviation from our current course and show on-screen."

"This will take a moment."

"I'll wait," Lena mumbled, relaxing into the chair, feeling in control for the first time in hours.

"Course on-screen."

She looked up, frowning at the confusing array of information. The new trajectory calculations appeared to reset the course but added another fifty years to the mission. Did she really want to be responsible for that decision?

"Computer, is this the only scenario for a course reset?"

"No. The other three hundred twenty-two permutations present as less statistically successful, even though they are more direct paths through the sector containing the spatial anomalies. This course correction has a three percent probability of success."

"Oh, God! Only three percent? Why?"

"The presence of spatial anomalies creates mathematical uncertainty with unknown variables that make calculation of successful course changes susceptible to error."

"Do any of the other course correction calculations take us away from the black holes, I mean spatial anomalies?" She had to use the right wording or else the computer would not know what she was asking.

"There are only four course calculations in this range. They each have a lower probability of success than the presented calculation. The highest probability in this set is point three-three percent."

"That's comforting. A three percent chance of surviving if we take the long way around, with no other options. Great."

"Lena." The spectral voice came back, stronger and louder than she'd heard it before.

She jumped. "Shit!" The ribbon of blue from the wall panel folded as another fine was added. "You're back."

"I'm sorry, it's getting harder for me to be in your

time."

"What do you mean, 'in my time'?"

"I'll answer your questions later if I can. You must take the longer route. Your life depends on it."

"But there's almost no chance the ship will survive if I set the course on that trajectory."

"It's the only course that gets you far enough away from the black holes. Trust me."

"But the computer . . ."

"The computer doesn't have all the information. It's been wrong every time we've tried to recalculate the detour." The echoing voice rumbled loudly around the bridge.

Lena bridled. "Now, just wait a freakin' minute! Why should I trust you?" she yelled. Then she registered the second part of what her ethereal companion had said. "Wait, what do you mean by 'every time'?"

There was an exasperated sigh that sounded like a barrel rolling in the cargo bay. "Lena, if you don't choose the long route, you'll be trapped here forever, endlessly trying to figure out a problem that can't be solved. Believe me, please. You and I have been through countless iterations of this exact moment already. I'm begging you to listen to me."

"Time loop aside—and we'll come back to it, I

promise—what you're asking me to do is suicide. I can't possibly trust you over the computer. If you aren't real, if you're just a figment of my imagination, how can I believe that any of this is actually happening?"

"I am real and trusting me *will* save your life. That is my oath to you." The voice faded again, the apparition more translucent and ephemeral.

"You're asking me to take a big leap of faith and we both seem to know that I am not a believer." Lena sat forward, resting her forehead in her hands. "Just because we've done this before and you say I've repeatedly chosen the wrong path, I am expected to trust you? I don't know you. I don't know what your game is."

"There is no game and soon the loop will be happening so fast we won't be able to escape it. Time is folding in on itself, and the closer the ship gets to the accretion disk of the first hole, the worse things get. I'm sure you can already feel how much warmer it is in here. Everyone on this ship is depending on you to make the course correction and take the wide trajectory."

Lena rose, crossed her arms and set her chin at a stubborn angle, suddenly aware that the bridge felt stuffy and hot. There was no doubt something was happening. She looked at the sensor readings. Hull temperature was up and reaching almost dangerous levels in some zones. Her determination stiffened. She wanted answers, reassurance for what her ghostly companion was telling her she had to do. "Let's say I believe you, and that we have little time left, I'm not doing anything until you tell me how this all started, and who you are."

The apparition swooped in, and a blanket of coolness descended over Lena, but she stood her ground. "Lena, you are so stubborn, but it's what will keep you alive." The old woman's face changed, and she looked sad, defeated even. "I know who you are because we are the same."

"How so?"

The old woman's misty gaze locked on Lena's. "I *am* you, and I got stuck here in this loop so long ago I can't even remember the exact details of it."

A cold certainty settled over Lena and she took a step back, denial slamming into her a second later.

SEVEN

The Loop

Lena was transfixed.

"I made the wrong choice and I lost everything. Thousands of times. Then something changed and I stepped outside of the loop. I thought that's when I'd be able to fix things, but it only got worse. Do you have any idea how exhausting it is to watch yourself go through the same agonizing mistakes, time after time, helpless to do anything about it?"

Lena shook her head, numb. This was unreal.

"It took everything I had to cross this veil, and I'm still trying to figure out how I do it. Sheer will, maybe? Faith? No idea." The old woman shrugged her sagging shoulders. "The only thing I know is that every time I do—and there have been so many attempts—it gets more and more difficult to do it again. All I have is you. And all I want is for you to have a little faith. For once."

"Faith? In you—I mean, me?" Lena could barely utter the words, her mind reeling at the improbabilities of it all, logic and reason losing their foothold with each passing moment.

"Faith in us. If we work together, this can all finally end. You need to follow the long-shot course. It's the only way to put everything right." The apparition was still, her diaphanous form filmy and thin. She seemed smaller and quieter. "Please, I'm begging you."

"All right. But I still have questions. You said something 'changed'. How do you know that wasn't you . . . creating some kind of time paradox?"

"I will try to answer your questions. Later. I'm not making any promises. There's something different about this loop that I must tell you about, and as I said, I've had a lot of trouble breaking through and speaking to you. That's new. If there's time, I will do my best to tell you what you want to know."

It was hard for Lena to believe she was staring back at a version of herself, and that she looked about eighty years older. She frowned, dragging her thoughts back to the task at hand—accept the instructions and reset the course. The old woman's tenacity impressed her and resonated deep in her psyche. It was a departure from the person she knew herself to be to blindly follow a gut response to the dire situation she was in. Perhaps there was a lesson in that. The choices she faced presented a double-jeopardy. One only she could resolve. Either adjust the course, risking everything for that three percent chance, or face certain oblivion.

"Computer, plot course nine-four-zero-two."

"Plotting."

Lena waited. The big view-screen refreshed and a glowing animation appeared, showing the *Vega Two* and its new course, plus additional data about the impact of the route changes.

"Approved. Make course correction on my mark. Three . . . two . . . one . . . mark."

"Course change initiated. Standby for starboard retrorocket burn one of ten."

The ship rumbled, and Lena braced through the increasing vibrations. Light bounced and shimmered off trembling surfaces. A deep creaking started in the bowels of the ship and became a chorus of material objections to the change in direction. Lena held on through every protesting shudder, the seat beneath her shaking until she was convinced even her bones rattled.

"Jeez, that's uncomfortable," she hissed, her quiet protest lost in the din.

The prolonged thruster burn brought her headache

back, the thumping resonance making her feel as if her head was in a vise. When the engine burn ceased, the quietness that came to rest around her was a relief.

"Oh, thank God that is over." The groaning deck settled, the silence slowly retreating behind the hum of computers running the new data sets to establish fresh journey parameters.

Lena glanced at the screen. A ship-wide diagnostic was ramping up—a full sweep for malfunctions, resets and corrections, identification of glitches and failures caused by the sharp vibrations. It was a standard automated process, and it gave Lena enough time to catch her breath and calm down.

She'd just committed the ship to an altered course change that took them decades outside of the original mission parameters and if it didn't work, everyone on the *Vega Two* was doomed.

"But I'm still the only one here." She knew it was unrealistic for the rest of the people on board the ship to suddenly appear as if nothing had happened, but she found it hard to be patient. If she understood even a fraction of the physics of black holes, it was that time behaved unpredictably and in unexpected ways. She half expected to be launched outside of her own time, worrying that this very moment was the one that cast old Lena from her own path into the endless loop she experienced.

"I am here too." The apparition glided into view, her hands clasped at her waist. "And there's a reason it's only the two of us. I made it happen."

This surprised Lena. Was it possible to make time stand still?

Suspicion creased her brow. "What? Why? What did you do with the rest of the ship's occupants?" She suddenly had a burning need to unravel the mystery around her solo occupation of the gigantic Ark-class ship.

"As far as I know, I am not responsible for everyone disappearing. I only did what I needed to do to be able to reach out to you. That is all I have control over—what happens to me, and by extension, to you." The apparition floated towards the screen, her back to Lena. "It is my understanding that I changed your timeline, and yours alone."

This was confusing. "Explain what you mean. Before, you said you stepped out of the loop and then tried to influence me." She stopped, the pain in her brow intense. "Well, other versions of me."

"Yes. It took me a while to realize I was outside of my time, the awareness only coming to me when I stumbled across another version of myself. Much like your earlier terror when you and I began to interact, I was scared out of my wits. I thought I was seeing a ghost."

Lena listened silently, empathizing with her older self.

"My initial experience was not like yours. At first, the ship was full of what appeared to be ghosts. I thought I had lost my mind. I was terrified. Those first loop backs, or time folds, made me question everything I knew. It took many loops to deduce that space-time had fractured. I was on a diverging path, moving away from the conventional time stream. My ghosts slowly disappeared until I was completely alone."

"Whoa." Lena thought back on how scared she had been and imagined how much worse it would have been to be surrounded by wraith-like apparitions. What struck her suddenly was that she had no trouble imagining what it was like. "I think—I don't know how— but I think I can remember . . ."

"It's possible. Maybe. Fractured time is not really my area of expertise." Old Lena sounded tired. Telling her story was draining her. "When I was alone, I thought I would die. I wanted to. I was close to suicidal when I almost ran straight into a version of myself in the concourse, getting drunk and trying not to lose it completely. From that moment, I focused on creating a link across the fractures to fix this mess."

"Well, we fixed it." Lena smiled apologetically.

"Yes. Finally. God, you don't know how long . . ." The old voice, thin and echoing, faded to stillness. A minute passed before she continued softly, "As I said, something about this loop is different. We altered something."

"Oh? Is that even possible?"

"There were a few timeline fluctuations before that gave me a clue that I could influence outcomes. I never took much notice, because they never changed the ultimate outcome."

"What did I do differently?" Lena was curious, sitting forward and straining to hear the faint voice over the computers.

"When you woke up on what you understand to be this morning, you were early. I think that was my doing. I had been working so hard on getting through to you, to nudge you awake somehow. I kind of lost my cool and may have screamed really, really close to your ear."

"And that somehow made a noticeable difference?"

"It made a massive difference. Every other time, when we arrived at the bridge, the crew were already busy correcting the course of the ship. In the previous loops, we slept a little longer at our desk, and things had always gone from bad to worse before there was a chance to do much about it.

"We were approaching the black holes, our speed increasing as we were pulled towards the accretion disk. Time compressed unexpectedly, robbing us of an opportunity to respond. The ship and everything; everyone on board suddenly disappeared."

Lena frowned, puzzled. If other Lena's ship had vanished, how was she here?

"Then it would start all over again. I believe the ship's caught in an eddy between the two accretion disks, kind of like being stuck in a taylor column. We keep reliving that moment because we are circling very close to the drain before getting spun back out. I've watched oblivion happen over and over, helpless to stop it."

"I am so sorry." Lena had a lump in her throat. The suffering of this older version of herself was unimaginable.

"All I had to do was wake up earlier."

"Well, you also had to connect to me. And what caused that to succeed is yet to be established, if we're ever able to work it out."

"It could be to do with how close our timelines are to each other on this loop. The eddy is probably breaking down. I knew I'd run out of loops sooner or later. I'm just glad it ends like this."

"So why, do you think, was everyone already gone in my loop?" Lena still couldn't understand this part. Perhaps she never would.

"I think it's possible it's another time fracture. You woke before the moment the original loop reset."

"Whoa."

"The saddest part for me is that what I experienced as mere moments were vast stretches of passing days, years, even decades. But then today has felt like years to me."

"And only hours for me," Lena finished the thought, her heart going out to the old woman.

"It took me far too long to realize I had to create a deviation in the loop." Old Lena glanced down at herself, ragged and crooked with the ravages of age. "I counted more than forty years from when I first woke up alone, but I could be way off. Time means nothing out here."

"I'm so sorry."

The woman approached, the coolness of her presence making the skin on Lena's arm pucker into goose flesh.

"I'm just happy my efforts finally succeeded. It has been a surprising bonus to have you for company. To be able to talk to you, have you *see* me. It has been so long since I've been seen." Her sorrow made her voice keen, like a high-pitched fan. "And we can see each other."

Lena sat back and grew pensive.

"So, you tried a few times to get through to me. Were all your attempts during what we have been referring to as 'this morning'?"

"Your morning, yes. Years for me. Although, I sense an acceleration over the past several hours. My time has begun to compress, and I fear we are swinging towards the event horizon side of the eddy once more."

Lena was alarmed. "But I changed the course. Won't that be enough to stop your time looping again?"

"I don't know. The ship still has all but one of its maneuvers to complete. You've succeeded in starting to nudge it back away from the holes. I wish I could tell you for sure that what we've done will work. I want to interrupt the cycle. All I can hope for is that what you are doing now will prevent you from going through what I've endured."

"I am grateful. Truly." Lena looked around. As

uncomfortable as her situation was, she had an uneasy realization. Her memories of this experience would be critical in avoiding a loop of her own. If old Lena's time could loop again, it stood to reason she wasn't out of trouble yet herself. It was suddenly urgent to know all the details of the other woman's efforts. "How did you know about the captain's key card in the briefing room table?"

"Remember I said there were fluctuations and differences in the courses of events I've experienced through the loops? Well, my original time was a little different than yours. Joe and I were together for a few months before the loops. It was all too brief and so long ago." She sounded sad.

"I dated the captain?" Lena squeaked, embarrassed at the flood of warmth on her face. "Isn't that against regulations?"

"Not in my timeline, and *I* dated the captain. You might still get your chance if this works."

The computer beeped. "Course modification burn two of ten initiating in thirty seconds. All hands to stations."

"Obviously, the computer doesn't know the ship's empty." Lena sat down again and held on for the bone-jarring shudder that came a moment later. The ship executed its course correction burn.

The big screen refreshed, indicating the beginnings of their deviated course. The red dotted line had separated from the solid blue line, marking their original course.

"Those burns should become less obvious as the ship follows the arc of the new trajectory. By number ten, you probably won't even know it's happening." Old Lena's voice was almost musical. The pitch had changed and she spoke faster.

"Something is happening to you."

"Time is changing. I can't stay for much longer."

"How will I know if this has all worked?"

"I'm hoping you don't loop and that the real flow of time merges you back with where you came from, as if none of this happened."

"Will I remember?"

"You must find a way. I made myself remember through creating recording, logs and notes. There was a residue of repetition that eventually stuck in my brain, but it took forever for me to sense the memories. After that, I moved away from the loop and watched versions of you doing the repeating."

"From outside of time." Lena returned to a nagging thought that bothered her about this scenario. "Now that I think about it, there are no rational answers for why you are here and able to speak to me. There is, however, another, more illogical explanation."

"I'm dead," old Lena said.

"You're dead."

EIGHT

A Little Faith

The involuntary prickle of fear down Lena's spine chilled her.

"That can't be right." She stared at the old woman, whose expression had become troubled.

"It can't be," Old Lena murmured, barely audible. She shook her head.

"However it transpired, the result is the same. You crossed over." Lena frowned. "My question is, why am I able to see you? I don't believe in ghosts. I don't believe in a spirit world."

"Maybe in the absence of all other forms of living energy, you are finally able to sense the energy I emit. My aura, my essence, became amplified because there is no other interference."

Lena gasped. "Then what we're really saying is the way you changed the loop was not by talking to me but by making that possible in the first place.

Your death changed my loop. Your energy is flowing into my timeline. With my loop devoid of life-forces besides my own, the silence has facilitated our ability to communicate. Fascinating."

They stared at each other. The unusual theory hung between them, fragile as the veil that separated them.

"It's what my mother—our mother—would call a miracle," Lena said

"Well, there's no scientific basis for what has happened, that much is true. I only know I had to do everything I could to get through to you."

"Unbelievable and remarkable. Now, let's see if your sacrifice will work." They both turned to look at the counter, the seconds sliding back towards the time the ship would execute another burn.

Old Lena drifted closer to her younger self, the coolness she brought with her now familiar. Lena looked at the craggy face.

"I wish I could hold your hand."

"That would be nice." The old woman's expression was sad, but she smiled anyway. "It's been so long since I felt the touch of another person."

"I wonder why everyone on your side is gone."

"For a long while, I've thought it was my time

fracture that tore me away from everyone else. But now, because we're entertaining implausible theories, perhaps it was for the same reason you are alone. I needed the silence to make my way to the pivotal moment at which I could cross over."

Lena's eyes blurred. It didn't sound implausible to her. It sounded like the only choice a lonely traveler could make after a lifetime of isolation. To end her life was the only act that would bring the old woman peace. Her heart clenched, making her chest ache.

"I'm sorry, Lena," she whispered to the old woman.

"If this works, I'm not."

"Thank you."

She smiled, the light returning to her eyes for a moment.

The computer chimed and the third burn shook the ship. Lena steadied herself in the captain's chair, waiting.

When the shudder from the engine burn eased, she glanced at the trajectory animation, the red line now quite distinct from the blue.

"Look, we're moving away from the black holes. It's working." Her excitement seemed out of place after so many hours of gnawing tension. She allowed herself a minute to savor it. "Lena?" she called and waited.

The old woman had disappeared again. It did not surprise her. Lena had grown quickly accustomed to the apparition wafting out of sight. The return of her older self caused less fear, even though she now understood the true nature of her visitor.

This would be an interesting conversation with her mother when things were back to normal. She wondered when that might be.

Another engine burn, a few hours later, came and went. Old Lena had been right. The shuddering of the first few burns had been the heaviest and most noticeable, the forces immense as the *Vega Two* worked to free herself from the gravitational field pulling her closer to the black holes. As they progressed, the engine burns became less intense, the vibrations reducing noticeably until they were nothing more than background turbulence.

When the apparition did not reappear, Lena grew worried. Had something happened to her, or had the thread holding their timelines together been severed when the ship moved away from the immense energy field of the swirling accretion disks that defined the anomaly in Sector B3?

It was impossible to know. The old theories espoused about the effects of black holes on time were numerous, and now as they traveled through space in their Ark-class ships, much of the science knowledge gained on Earth was ancient. With little capability to expand on what they knew of space and time from those old theories, the Vega mission had been launched on the hopeful notion that life would prevail through their efforts, and that one day, science would again reach beyond the immediacy of human understanding and explore the improbable and unknown. In the meantime, they put a lot of stock in faith to bridge their knowledge gaps.

And I guess faith is good enough for now. The Vega mission is about trusting in ourselves, and others, thought Lena as she strolled around the bridge checking the various workstations.

A scratching sound started soon after the sixth burn. It was soft at first, but quite distinct in the heavy silence, broken only by the whine of computer fans.

A shape shot across the bridge above Lena's head and she cried out in alarm, startled by it.

The noise came from the shadows in the ceiling maze of conduits. Then a small bird flew down and perched on the navigation console and chirped.

Lena jumped, then burst out laughing, scaring the bird. It took off, escaping the bridge through the doors

Lena had left open.

She yawned, suddenly exhausted. The bird's unexpected appearance had broken the focus she'd maintained for many hours until the small creature disturbed her work. By her calculations, she'd been awake for over twenty-three hours, most of that time in a perpetual state of high anxiety. She was worn out and decided that after the next burn in two hours, she would go and sleep. There was little else she could do.

She was thankful for the sparrow, even though it had startled her. It was a sign that things were returning to normal on the *Vega Two*. Her current timeline appeared to be merging with the one she had been removed from by the strange events of the past day. She still didn't know how it had all happened and she was nervous for when the captain returned with questions about their new course and the changes to the mission.

"I'll have to work on something after my nap. I just wish old Lena was here to help me explain things."

She waited, half expecting her vocalization of her thoughts to conjure the ghostly presence the way it had before.

Nothing happened and she continued through the concourse towards the residential zone. Birds flitted above her head and she sighed. She spotted a butterfly.

Signs of life that had been missing for most of the day. She couldn't help the smile that crept over her features. Unlike the moment she had sensed a presence when old Lena had appeared, Lena knew she wasn't alone anymore. It felt good.

She tried not to get too excited, tempering her impatience. It could take a long time for everything to return to normal. The emergence of her previous timeline could not be fully trusted because she had no way of knowing if the progress back towards that path would continue, or if a loop would spontaneously return her to where, and when, she'd started the day, alone and afraid.

That thought deflated her somewhat and her mind drifted back to the old woman. Even as old Lena had failed to correct her own path, she'd averted a similar fate in this time loop.

"Well, maybe let's not put too much stock in a few small creatures reappearing."

NINE

Unexpected Outcome

Her device chimed, and Lena rolled over.

You're going to be late! Get up, Lena.

The message wrenched her from the fog of sleep, and she bolted out of her bed, suddenly alert. Her heart raced and she took big gulps of air.

"It worked! Jesus, it actually worked." A blue fine appeared out of the panel on the wall, and she flicked the paper with one finger before she grabbed it and stuffed it in her pocket.

She stopped to check her watch, coming more fully awake as her stress levels rose. The dramatic events of the previous day were still on her mind when she tucked a flop of dark hair behind her ear.

She froze.

"How long have I been asleep?" Time had changed; altered, along with her hair, which was now shoulder length. She'd had a buzz cut the previous morning when she woke at her desk.

She shook her head, pulling on her uniform and trying to whittle down her preparations because she really was going to be late. *So much for taking a short nap,* she thought.

The message on her device had been from her friend, Vince. He knew her well, and she couldn't help but grin. Her excitement at being back among the living gave her energy to spare, and she jogged from the residential zone and into the concourse, now brimming with life.

"Ha!" Lena exclaimed, her arms flung wide. She ignored the startled glances from passersby, lost in her happiness.

"Lena, come over here." Vince waved at her, the frown of disapproval on his face making her grin spread.

She ran over and hugged him tightly. "How the hell are you, buddy?"

"Uh . . . are you quite well in the head?" Her friend pushed her back, keeping a hold on her shoulders as he studied her closely.

"I'm good. Better than good. I'm great." The etiquette bot had rolled up and waved her fine at her.

She grabbed it and shoved it in the pocket of her pants along with the other two fines she'd already been issued for her spontaneous and effervescent outbursts.

"Lena, I'm worried about you. You've been working so hard lately. I think you need a furlough."

"Nonsense. What I need is to get to work. Drinks after?"

"Positively. I'll see you at eight?"

"As usual. Thanks for the wakeup call. I needed it today." She sauntered off, embracing her fresh start with undisguised enthusiasm.

At the bridge, she climbed off the elevator into the bustling hum of activity. She suppressed a giddy snicker, certain it would draw the ire of the second shift commander who was currently scrolling data on the control panel of the captain's chair.

She glanced at the main display monitors. Everything appeared to be normal. Exactly as expected. There seemed to be no hangovers from her timeline divergence and subsequent merge.

"Good morning, sir." She greeted Commander Morris, who dipped his chin without looking up from his reading.

Lena's morning proceeded without incident and when her shift ended, she left the bridge with a smile on her face. She was grateful for the return to business as usual. No one looked out of place, no one questioned her about the past few days, and nothing out of the ordinary occurred to indicate all was not well with the *Vega Two*.

She was settling into her new-found appreciation for the status quo when her device chimed a reminder. She glanced at the screen, expecting it to be a message from Vince, reminding her of their hangout later. Instead, she read the note about a haircut appointment, set for twenty minutes from now.

Lena stopped dead in her tracks, a cold wave of dread making her shiver.

"Damn it." The fine joined the others.

She had felt so secure in the predictability and smooth march of routine through the day that she'd failed to notice something very crucial.

It was an exact replica of the day prior to them spotting the anomaly; and two days before she'd found herself alone on the bridge with a ghost of herself.

Time had looped. And it looked like it had gone even further back than either she or Old Lena had predicted. They'd assumed she'd only be repeating the same day, as in all the other loops before the one that changed everything.

"And that's where the problem is. *We changed everything.*" She ground out the words through a clenched jaw. "God knows what happens now."

She'd forgotten about the day before the dramatic events surrounding the discovery of the black holes, and although things had felt vaguely familiar, she'd dismissed it, believing that sense of sameness was due to being back in her own time.

The haircut that was scheduled for twenty minutes from now was the one at which she'd shorn her hair for charity, the result of which was the tidy crew-cut she'd woken with the day they'd discovered the black holes.

"Christ Almighty, what the fuck am I supposed to do now?"

Two etiquette bots rolled up. "Attention, you have been found in violation of etiquette code six-fourteen, dash two. You are remanded into our custody and will proceed directly to the brig. Failure to comply will result in additional time on your sentence." The commanding voice of the robot drew glances from the crowd gathered near the elevator. One or two people looked annoyed, most just looked sympathetic.

"I need to talk to the captain," Lena demanded in a firm voice as she walked ahead of the bots.

"Your request is denied."

"Why?"

"Your request cannot be fulfilled at this time."

"No, I guess you wouldn't understand." She thought for a moment. "I need to speak to Commander Philips."

"Commander Philips will be with you shortly for your arraignment."

Philips was the senior officer in charge of enforcement.

"Good."

Lena stepped over the threshold of the holding cell. It was a narrow space with a bunk and a toilet which stood behind a half wall for the pretense at privacy. She sneered. This was a problem.

If she couldn't convince Philips that she needed to speak to the captain, the ship would head for the black hole and she'd be helpless to do anything because she'd wake up in this cell tomorrow, and everyone else would be gone.

Or would they? She was so confused. She sat down and thought hard about where she was in time, relative to when she'd discovered she was alone.

Two days. *It is the day after tomorrow when I wake up alone.* "Not tomorrow." But that didn't solve her current dilemma. "I might be in here just long enough to make it impossible to fix things."

She couldn't understand how she'd arrived further back in her timeline. She'd looped back by *two days*— much earlier than she'd expected she would. Her fear was that this change could alter her time loops irrevocably. What if she wasn't be able to get out of the brig? What if Old Lena never showed up? And even if she did, would there be anything they could do if she was stuck in a cell?

The small room was enclosed by a thick plexiglass. She could see out and down the passage, and that was all. Lena paced, contemplating her current and future fates.

An hour passed. Then another, and another. It was evening before the door opened and she was escorted from the cell to a claustrophobic chamber where a disciplinary panel was already seated and waiting. Commander Philips sat in the middle. On either side of him were his junior lieutenants. They would decide Lena's punishment.

"Lieutenant Dixon . . ." He read the report of her outburst. When he looked up, a frown etched his brow. "I see you have several language and outburst infractions. All from today. Has something happened to precipitate your change in behavior, lieutenant?" He seemed a patient and open-minded man, and she decided she had to appeal to him to get an audience with the captain.

"Sir, I apologize. I've been under duress today. I have information that the captain needs to hear urgently. Is there any way I could speak with him directly?"

He leveled an appraising look at her, sitting back in his chair. Philips was a few years off retirement. He'd run a disciplined and well-behaved ship. Punishments had been commensurate with the offenses under his watch. Lena didn't know of anyone who had a complaint about the commander. Knowing all this did not make it any easier to bear his intense scrutiny. His stern gaze made her squirm inwardly.

"Dixon, I don't believe you are in a position to be asking me for favors."

"I understand, sir, but my request is to ensure the safety of the Vega Two."

"Are you threatening the safety of this vessel, lieutenant?"

"No, sir! Absolutely not, sir. But I must speak with the captain. New data has come to light about this region of space and it is my duty to inform the captain, sir."

He contemplated her for a moment, a deep frown

darkening his expression before he leaned over to consult with his lieutenants.

"You are a pilot, yes?"

"Yes, sir."

"Not a navigator."

"No, sir. Please, the ship is in danger." She gulped. The commander's rising suspicion made her doubt her ability to convince him they needed to act quickly. "If I could just have a moment of the captain's time, everything will be explained."

He sighed and turned to his panel. They muttered among themselves for a few moments, then one of the lieutenants shrugged, throwing a glance at her. She prayed for her chance to speak to the captain. But that was only part of her plan. She had to convince him of the course change to bypass sector B3, which would be a most significant challenge, considering what it meant. Her thoughts strayed to the pushed-out timeline. Fifty more years . . .

Her reverie was interrupted when Commander Philips turned to address her. "I will see what I can do about getting you in front of the captain. In the meantime, your punishment is a fine of five thousand credits and three days of community service, to begin at the end of your next shift. Dismissed."

She was taken back to the cell to await the captain's reply to her request.

The hours seemed to drag as she waited. The irony of each passing minute was not lost on her and she swore never to waste or take for granted the gift of more time.

"That's if I can convince the captain not to steer us straight at the event horizon of a black hole," she mumbled under her breath.

The door at the far end of the corridor opened, and the captain thanked the sentry on duty, turning his gaze on her.

"It's like I can summon them with my thoughts. I have superpowers." The man strode towards her, and she suppressed a grin. She remembered what old Lena had told her about her relationship with the captain—Joe—and felt a flood of heat rise to her cheeks. Embarrassed that the romantic notion of them together caused a quiet thrill, she dug her fingernails into her palms and forced herself to adopt a professional demeanor. The captain stopped outside her cell, a guard joining him to open a small hatch in the door.

She stood to attention, snapping a crisp salute at the man on the other side of the glass, his hands behind his back.

Memories of being in his private quarters flashed in Lena's mind. She stared over his head unable to meet his direct and serious gaze.

"At ease, lieutenant. I understand you wanted to speak with me urgently."

"Yes, sir."

"Give me a minute." He disappeared. A moment later, the locks on the cell were released, and the door swung open.

Lena waited. The captain reappeared and gestured for her to come out. She fell into step beside him, noticing his features were set in an unreadable mask. He was good at hiding his feelings. It was a requirement of the post. The captain had to have a steady hand and cool head.

"Now, what is it you wanted to tell me?"

"Sir, I'd prefer if I could show you. I suspect we are headed for danger, which we will need to act quickly to avoid."

"Really? What kind of danger?"

"As I said, I think it would be better if I showed you." She insisted before remembering her rank. "Sir."

A smile played at the corner of his mouth. "Very well. Where to?"

"The bridge, sir."

"Lead the way, lieutenant."

They strode across the concourse, the smell of fresh bread and other food aromas reaching Lena. She'd been so absorbed with the black hole problem that she'd not eaten throughout her entire ordeal. To echo the thought, her stomach growled noisily.

"Have you eaten anything yet? I believe you were apprehended straight after your shift."

"Yes, sir." She swallowed, embarrassed. "I can't recall when last I ate."

"Can your urgent problem wait a few more minutes, lieutenant?"

Her stomach growled again, and her head swirled. She was running on fumes. "I guess it could, captain. I apologize."

"No need. It's been a long day." He directed her towards a coffee shop that served sandwiches with its delicious hot beverages.

The server perked up and helped Lena choose some food and a drink.

"Just water?" The captain smiled. "The coffee here is expensive, but I promise, I can afford it."

Lena felt the blush rise. He was being very charming and she had a distinct impression that this was that moment for her. She smiled, wondering if old

Lena could see her. "Thank you, sir, but all I want is the water."

"If you insist." He nodded at the server, who keyed in the order and prompted an on-screen bill that the captain added to his tab. "There's a table. Sit and eat, and maybe give me the summary of what we are going to be looking at when we get to the bridge."

She sat down opposite him and took a few sips of water, wondering where she should start. He seemed intent on knowing something of what was going on before she was able to show him her evidence. With no way around his persistence, she arranged her thoughts while she chewed a mouthful of food.

"Captain, something unusual is out there. Our current course is pointing us almost straight at it, and—don't ask me to tell you how I know this—the day after tomorrow, we will make a course alteration that will put the Vega Two at serious risk."

"This is the first I'm hearing of any problems." He looked thoughtful. "Are you sure we are going to encounter an issue?"

"I am, sir. The reason we haven't detected any anomalies is because we're not seeing any yet. The ones we encounter are not visible to our sensors at this range."

"Then I'm interested to see what you can show me when we get to the bridge." He sat back and Lena ate quickly. She choked down the sandwich, her anxiety and discomfort preventing her from enjoying the food or the company.

"Done?" Captain Mallory asked, half out of his chair already.

"Yes. Thank you." Lena rose, again remembering too late that this was the captain she was speaking to. "Sir," she added belatedly.

"It's okay, Lena. When it's just the two of us, you can drop the captain bit."

"Oh." Her mouth formed the shape of the sound, her brain confounded by the removal of formality.

"To be honest, I'm glad we're having a chance to talk today. I've been wanting to do this for a while, but could never quite find the courage to break the ice."

Lena's eyes widened. The captain needed courage to talk to her? Yes, this had to be the moment.

"Sir, I am flattered. I didn't realize."

"Well, I hope we can take another shot at a meal together when we're off duty. With so few of us on this ship, we need to make connections wherever possible, don't you think?" He smiled, a casual expression with no subtext. He was being friendly. She found she liked it. She liked him. He was not what she'd expected. Everyone on board had been the same to her, making barely an impression on her with their bland uniformity. Until now. It excited her to find someone who intrigued her.

Lena nodded, unable to verbalize her agreement to the open invitation, still confused about the apparent lack of regulations that prevented fraternization among crew. She'd always thought it was against the rules. If the captain was willing to cast the regs aside, who was she to object?

The captain led the way out of the coffee shop. She glanced around, wishing for once to see the other Lena appear so she could throw her old self a quiet high five. To her disappointment, she had to refrain from her celebrations, because the crowded concourse bore no trace of the woman's ghostly presence. *Too much living energy,* she mused silently, disappointed.

Lena shook her head, her racing mind a distraction from what she needed to focus on. It occurred to her that the captain's handsome smile could soon be gone. *We may never get to share a meal, or anything else, if I can't get this ship on its new course.*

At the bridge, the bosun's whistle signaled and the shift commander rose from the captain's chair.

"Captain on the bridge," Commander May announced. The first-shift crew rose to attention.

"As you were. Nav, we need your console."

"Yes, sir." The lieutenant vacated her seat and waited to one side.

"Right. Show me." Captain Mallory gestured for Lena to take the seat.

She sat, turning towards the controls. "Sir, I don't have clearance for the search I want to do. Would you mind?"

"Of course. Computer, clearance code panel." He reached over and typed in his captain's code and the console's lighting went from light gray to blue. A quick biometric scan of his thumb activated his authorization code, and the screen went gray again.

Why hadn't she needed the biometrics when she'd changed course in her previous loop? Perhaps that was one of those differences old Lena had been talking about. Lena glanced at the captain, thinking for the first time that this wasn't her old timeline, but a new one, branched off out of their alterations to the loop in which the two women had worked together to save the ship. She swallowed hard. Did it really matter? She was here now, and she still had to save the *Vega Two*.

Lena plotted a radio burst and set the range. "Sir,

when I send this signal at those coordinates, you'll see what I mean. It could take a minute to illustrate my point, considering the target distance."

"Go ahead, lieutenant."

The commander and navigator had drifted closer, curious to see what Lena was doing.

She touched the command switch, and a long-wave radio signal was sent from the huge dish on the bow of the ship. They watched the render of an animation that tracked the signal in real time. A few minutes passed and the signal looked steady until it wobbled, then disappeared.

"Why did it disappear?" The communications ensign asked. There was a small crowd behind the chair now.

"There's only one reason a radio signal would disappear." The captain straightened, crossing his arms and staring at the big screen.

"A black hole," finished the navigator, her face a mask of worry. "Can I sit?" She directed the question at Lena.

"Of course." Lena got up and retreated from the group that was closing around the navigator.

The woman's hands flew over the console, preparing another set of instructions. "Execute render," she said quietly. The screen went blank for a second before a fresh animation appeared depicting the *Vega Two* and what looked like a small black hole within a few million kilometers of its current course.

"Time to intercept?" asked the captain, his voice tight.

"Roughly four days, but the clock's already acting strangely. It keeps changing."

"There's two of them."

Everyone turned to look at Lena.

"What? How do you know?" The captain's worried expression deepened.

"I detected what I believe is a second one just beyond the first. They are converging."

"Christ," someone muttered, a blue slip slid from the etiquette monitoring panel on the wall.

For a minute, the crew stood, absorbing the information before the room erupted into a frenzy of activity.

The captain relieved the shift commander and sat in the big chair at the center of the bridge. He scanned the screen to his left as various crew members worked to gather data about the black holes. Lena retreated to a corner of the room, unsure of what to do next.

"Lieutenant, take a seat. I may need you again." He

gestured to the bench against the wall behind her.

"Yes, captain." Lena nodded, still not sure what she could possibly assist him with.

"Do we have a new scenario render yet? I want to see what we're dealing with." The command seemed to galvanize the already busy crew. The noise level on the bridge grew.

"Ready, captain," the science officer, Commander Salah, spoke over the din. "On-screen now."

The big screen refreshed to show the now-familiar image of the two black holes, and Lena swallowed hard, then sank onto the bench. This couldn't be happening. She looked away, desperately wishing this wasn't real.

"Okay. What now, captain?" The question came from the navigation officer.

"We have to plot possible scenarios for intercept, find a way around this thing that will do the least amount of damage to the ship and to the mission."

Minutes passed as if in a blur, Lena quietly observing the focus of a crew dealing with the imminent crisis. The screen refreshed.

"It won't work," Lena blurted, alarm causing her to leap to her feet. She recognized the plotted line the navigator had just rendered onto the animation. It was the solid blue line that had led to the timeline rift she had experienced. Her words were lost in the din and she collected her courage.

She strode towards the captain's chair and put a hand on his arm. He turned, surprised by the unexpected contact.

"Lena," he forgot himself, momentarily distracted by her presence.

"Sir, it won't work. That scenario." She pointed at the screen.

"Captain, I disagree." The navigator swiveled in her chair to challenge Lena's statement. "If we ride the outer wave of the accretion disk of the first hole, we can skim past both of them if we execute a retro burn as we reach the apex of the maneuver." She sounded confident.

"It doesn't work." Lena became insistent.

The captain's gaze was steady and he gave her a nod. "What is your suggestion?"

"Sir, with respect, she's not a navigator. Why are you asking her?"

"The lieutenant has earned some leeway here, Lieutenant Kane. I want to hear what she thinks." He turned to Lena. "Go ahead."

"The problem is the second black hole's forces on the accretion disk of the first make that move unpredictable. I believe it will interfere with our course correction and begin to scramble time before we are able to steer out of the combined gravitational field. There's an eddy—" she stopped, unsure of how to proceed, then changed what she was about to say, "—there's a chance there's a gravitational eddy in the area between the holes. We could end up stuck there, unable to escape and slowly getting dragged over the event horizon as the holes merge." She straightened, emboldened by the captain's impressed expression. A small smile turned up the corner of his mouth, and he nodded.

"Nav, look for gravitational eddies around the black holes, please, then calculate the probability of hitting one of them if we complete that course correction."

The navigator huffed and swung back to her station, her hands flying. A few moments later, she sent a new render to the big screen. They watched, all a bit horrified, to see the scenario play out exactly as Lena predicted.

"Shit." The captain rubbed his chin. "What do you suggest?" He was trusting her now, completely depending on her to provide the answer. The shift commander crumpled the blue slip and shoved it in his pocket.

"We only have one option. We recalculate and take the long way around."

TEN

No Time to Lose

The bridge was silent. Everyone waited, watching as the captain and Lena, their gazes locked, squared off over her latest bombshell. She swallowed. Captain Mallory's expression changed from trust to suspicion, then anger.

"Nav, hold course until I get back."

"Aye, captain." Kane swiveled in her chair and focused on her controls. The room resumed the normal level of activity.

"Briefing room. Now," the captain ordered, his voice crisp and low.

Lena flinched. The moment had come to reveal what she knew, and how she knew it.

"Aye, captain." Her mouth was dry and her stomach did flip-flops. The next moments would determine the fate of the *Vega Two*. She had to choose her words carefully.

"Commander May, you have the ship." The captain had risen from his chair and strode towards the briefing room, the door sliding open silently. He did not wait to see if Lena was behind him, and she followed, her pulse racing.

A memory of prying those doors apart flashed in her mind. She walked through into the briefing room, appreciating the privacy of the space. To his credit, the captain had not demanded an explanation right there, on the bridge, in front of his whole command crew.

Captain Mallory paced at the far end of the table, rubbing his chin and glancing at her from time to time. "You're not kidding, are you?" He shook his head. "The plan you're suggesting puts us at risk of mission failure, and yet I sense you are dead serious."

"Sir, it's the only course of action where there's any chance of succeeding. If we adjust course to what's out there, on that screen, we'll be pulled into a black hole and cease to exist. At least if we deviate far enough from the plotted course, we have time to plan and execute for a recovery that will help secure the mission long term." Lena's pulse pounded in her temples. They were so close to making it out of this alive, if only the captain would hold his nerve.

"Explain."

"Sir?"

"How do you know all of this? I'm not an idiot, Lena. I can see the data, and what it's telling me, but there's more to this, isn't there? You knew there were two black holes. Before we did a scan for the second one. You knew the course adjustment wouldn't work, that there is a gravitational eddy. How?"

She took a deep breath. "I doubt you'll believe me, but I've been through this all before. For whatever reason, and don't ask me to explain it because I don't know, I am stuck in a time loop."

"What?" His confusion was etched into his expression.

"Captain, my time has looped back on itself, and possibly fractured. I don't know for sure." She blinked, plunging in. "All I know is, I am going to wake up and spend the whole of what will be Wednesday—day after tomorrow—completely alone on this ship. I will try to figure out how to stop us from getting wiped out by a black hole we only discovered on the Tuesday in my original timeline. I know all this because it's already happened to me, and if we go near the anomaly, it will happen again." Her voice cracked and she struggled to maintain her composure.

He stared at her, disbelief replacing his confusion.

"We have to turn the ship away from the black holes or we will all die. I will spend a whole day trying to get into the system to change the ship's course and probably fail. Over and over again." He was shaking his head, and her desperation peaked. She grappled for some tangible evidence—anything—and her eyes caught sight of his reflection on the table between them.

"Captain, you keep your backup of the command codes on a card in a hidden compartment." She walked to the head of the long table and put her hand on the shallow indent. "Here." Lena pressed the dimple. The secret panel with small drawers rose silently up from the gleaming table.

"How did you—"

"The same way I know that there's a bottle of prescription pain meds on your bathroom vanity next to your shaver." It was a personal detail she was hesitant to share, but it was necessary. It would convince him of the authenticity of her strange tale, she was sure.

He stared at her for what felt like several minutes, then walked around the chairs on the far side of the table. Lena watched him, pensive and afraid.

"A whole day by yourself on this ship?" His tone

gave nothing away.

"Well, not exactly." His eyebrow shot up, and she quickly validated. "There was a . . . ghost."

"Lena."

She put up a hand, and he stopped, crossed his arms, and waited. "Time becomes unpredictable when you're within range of a black hole. I'm sure you've noticed the glitches in your perception of the passage of minutes and hours, the strange repetition of events, like déjà vu, but not. Well, I had the pleasure of—actually, at first, I was terrified—but, I met an older version of myself because time, that close to the accretion disk of a black hole, does not work how you expect it to."

He shook his head but remained quiet.

"Older Lena scared the bejeezuz out of me when she first appeared. Long story short—and I can always give you the long version if we survive this—she explained how she and I were able to communicate. She spliced my timeline, and the reality in which she could communicate with me formed."

"The empty ship."

"Yes. We figured out that she also needed to have the same situation on her side—the empty ship—to reach across from her side to mine. She spent forty years like that, attempting to figure out how to get back to the moment things went wrong until she . . ." Lena's voice drifted.

"She died." The captain came to stand in front of her. "Is that how you finally were able to see her?"

She nodded, unable to speak.

"Well, then it was a miracle, because I haven't seen you in the chapel in years." His smile was gentle. "I am a man of faith; kind of have to be to run this ship. I believe that not everything has a logical explanation, and I also believe in my crew. Your track record speaks for itself, so I want to put my faith in you and your story."

Lena looked up, locking her gaze with his. "I know I sound delusional, but everything I've told you has one purpose. I want to save the ship. All I'm asking is that you believe me now. Taking the long route is the only way we survive. The older version of me spent decades eliminating all the other possibilities."

Captain Mallory regarded her for a moment, his expression changing little. Finally, he said, "Come on." He guided her out of the briefing room, the doors gliding open to admit the noise from the bridge. The bosun's whistle sounded and he relieved the commander of the con.

"Sir, orders?" Commander May asked. The crew

grew quiet, waiting on the captain.

"Lieutenant Kane, revise our course to avoid sector B3."

"Aye, captain," the navigator said, her hands working steadily at her controls. "Calculating the new course now."

The bridge crew watched in tense silence. They were about to make a major change and they would always be known for having executed the orders that changed the fate of the Vega Two, for better or for worse.

"Course correction calculated, captain," Lieutenant Kane said.

"Initiate."

"Aye, captain." Kane looked up, wearing a quizzical expression. "Don't you want to check the correction first, sir?"

"Really no point, is there, Kane? We're still going to go that way." Captain Mallory shrugged. Lena was impressed. His confidence immediately put the crew at ease and the tension in the room dissipated.

"Alert, course change authorization required." The computer refreshed the screen, showing the *Vega Two's* new path through the star system, skirting the black holes, taking them off their original course.

The captain tapped the console before the quick scan of his thumb. "Look" he said, smiling at Lena.

She glanced at the screen she'd tried to avoid, for fear of the data she already guessed would appear. Decades of additional travel time was ahead of them, and she was responsible. But what they saw could hardly be believed.

The crew buzzed with excitement. Someone clapped. The new course added only eleven years to their journey. "What the hell?" Lena breathed. A fine appeared in the wall console.

"I'll take that," the captain said. Her fine was passed to him and was duly crumpled up.

"Something changed again."

"What do you think it was?" he asked in a low voice so the others couldn't overhear their conversation.

Lena stared at the screen, lost in thought, retracing her steps through this current time. Her eyes grew wide, and she turned to smile at the captain. "I looped back to two days before my solo day."

"And?"

"We addressed the problem a whole day earlier than in the previous time loops. That means we're not subject to the accretion disk's gravitational forces yet, we haven't started to accelerate yet, and the course correction is happening now, not," she stopped to add up the hours, "over thirty-six hours from now."

"Well, then I think we caught a lucky break." He winked at her and relaxed back into his chair. "There's something else I believe in—luck."

He nodded, and they watched the computer process the new commands, displaying new trajectory information in real time as the upcoming engine burns were calculated. The first burn began as the data finished filling the screen. The deck shuddered underfoot, and Lena took a deep breath. They had saved the ship. With every passing moment, she felt more sure of that fact.

"Now that we know this maneuver isn't a complete disaster, can I get some options for as wide a berth as possible around the anomaly? I want to make certain there is no danger from the black holes."

"Aye, captain." Kane input information and the computer rolled out data on the screen. A rendering appeared, the animation showing the distinct arc the ship would take to avoid the black holes plus two other paths that took the ship to within range of the outer effects of the gravitational well.

"There are two alternative route options that add fifteen years and four months, or thirteen years and eight months."

"Thank you, Kane."

Lena looked from the screen to the captain. He was deep in thought. There was a lot to do to balance out the alteration in the length of the *Vega Two's* journey time.

"Captain, I think we should avoid the lesser time options, and go for the longest and widest berth. We don't know what this thing is going to do, and we don't want to be anywhere near it if those holes merge." She was cautious with her advice, knowing full well she had no authority to be advising Captain Mallory, except on the grounds of her recent experience. Everything they did from this moment on was not within her ability to know the outcome of. It was all new, and she was aware she was leaning heavily on his favorable response to her previous entreaties. "Fifteen years is doable. Crews can plan for resources to stretch, diligent ship's maintenance can extend the life of the *Vega Two*, population dynamics can be reworked."

He nodded, a thoughtful expression making his gaze distant. "It will be months of additional work, but I think you're right. It's what my grandmother used to call a speed bump."

"Sir?"

"Old Earth thing because they had roads on the

surface people used to drive vehicles on. A speed bump slowed a person down." He pointed at the screen. "*That is our speed bump.*"

Lena smiled and nodded. A deadly speed bump, but she got the analogy.

Captain Mallory sighed again. "Lieutenant, your work here is done. Go and get some rest."

Lena dipped her chin, checking the big screens one last time, still unsure of this reality. She felt disconnected and like a trespasser. It would take some getting used to. Her body ached and her exhaustion made her mind cloudy and bowed her frame. It would be good to take a break and rest.

"Aye, captain."

She left the bridge and headed for her quarters. When she entered the bustling concourse, she was greeted with familiar sounds and smells, all of which had been absent through her ordeal. Relief made the smile linger on her lips.

The ship felt alive, present, and thriving. She had helped make that happen. Her older self had worked so hard to communicate the danger of the black holes to her, for which she would always be grateful. They had made a good team when she'd eventually put aside her own fears.

She wondered what had happened to old Lena. How had she died? When had she died? Where was she now? There would always be more questions than answers about the curious intersection of their timelines and the events of the day out of time that she alone had lived to see.

"Lena!"

A happy smile spread across her face. "Hey, Vince." She stopped to wait for her friend. Vince was a welcome intrusion on her fatigue. He trotted over, bringing with him the aroma of fresh-baked bread.

She closed her eyes for a moment, reveling in the smell. The familiar comfort of it made her doubts and worries evaporate, and the heavy cloak of her recent trauma fell away.

"I see you missed your haircut," he said, fluffing her still long brown hair.

"Yeah, something came up. I'll reschedule." It wouldn't take a lot to get back on track, both in her life and on board the ship she called home.

"Well, it better have been important. That challenge is part of the opening events for the kids' center." Despite his stern words, he was smiling. He made it sound more serious than it was, but Lena's perceptions had altered. She'd agreed to the challenge because it had sounded like fun at the time. Now she felt a deep responsibility to do everything she could to participate more actively in the lives of the children on the *Vega Two.* She'd saved them from oblivion. Every day they lived from now on was a gift, and their great grandchildren would, one day, step off this ship and into a new world.

Without warning, she reached over and hugged her friend, almost knocking Vince off balance.

"Whoa! Easy, Len. What was that for?" he asked when she stepped out of his arms.

"Nothing. I just needed a hug. It feels like ages since I had one." She shrugged, a little embarrassed.

"Anytime you need a hug, you know where to find me. Lots of hugs to look forward to." His brown eyes twinkled, bringing to mind another pair of eyes.

She wondered what a hug from Captain Joe Mallory would feel like, and a delicious thrill of anticipation washed over her.

ELEVEN

A New Day

When she woke the next morning, it was to the news that she would be receiving a commendation for her actions. She would be receiving an award for her work on the black hole problem, and a promotion to full rank. The day passed as any other, as did the next— the day she had dreaded for fear of finding herself alone again. Instead, it ended with dinner plans with the captain.

When the glassware on their table tinkled unexpectedly, she couldn't resist glancing around, noticing a shimmer of light dancing at the edge of her sight.

"Just a retrorocket firing, Lena." Joe reached over and tucked her hand into his.

Lena suspected it was something more, a smile spreading across her face at the belief that her older self was finally at peace. Back in the moment, she absorbed the delightful warmth of Joe's hand cradling hers, his fingers stroking the back of her wrist. There was so much comfort in that one caress, and happiness settled over her. A vision of the years to come stretched out ahead, her future like a dream manifested.

Yes, she had a lot to look forward to in this second-chance reality.

Dear Reader,

Thank you for reading **Ghost of Time**. I hope you enjoyed this novella. Please remember that authors rely on reviews and every reader that leaves one is helping other readers choose the books they will enjoy. I hope you review **Ghost of Time** where you purchased it and on Goodreads.com

Cheryl Lawson,
Author

More from Cheryl Lawson.

The Journey to Vega Series of novellas: **A Dark Genesis** and **Erebus.**

A Dark Genesis: A cascade of horrifying events occur after a deep space asteroid strike. Sage, Noah and Dylan have little time to prove the crystalline form taking over their ship is a parasitoid entity. Things get all too real as friends succumb to the blooming and systems go critical. Is the cost of saving the Vega Four too high?

Erebus: A series of mysterious accidents aboard the Vega Six is no coincidence. The investigation, conducted by Rix Flowers, Cal Epps and Bass Decker uncovers an ancient and deadly foe who has a score to settle. Can Erebus, the primordial gatekeeper of darkness, be stopped or will he succeed in exacting his terrible toll?

The Rubicon Saga books: **We Are Mars, Storm At Dawn, Break the Dark.**

Series description: Mars is home to Rubicon, an intrepid science mission made up of two factions—g-mods and non-gens. Tensions run high across the class divide, but their petty disagreements soon pale into insignificance when they're faced with a series of disturbing and deadly disasters and challenges.

Separating the weak from the strong; the brave from the timid and the loyal Mars settlers from the traitors, forces beyond their control test the bonds of love, friendship and duty. Get swept along with Dana, Jaxon, Lenny, Chuck, Zane, Swift and Toni as they traverse the unforgiving Mars landscape, dive deep into its underground labyrinths and fight for their survival against the odds, and against enemies known and unknown.

We Are Mars, Storm At Dawn and Break the Dark are the epic and thrilling books of the **Rubicon Saga.** Each story brings you adventure, excitement, intrigue, romance and a cast of incredible characters who must fight to survive, to live and love on a far off and hostile world.

Available in ebook and paperback from book sellers, including Amazon.

FIND Cheryl online at:

Website: **cheryllawson.net**

Instagram: **cheryl_lawson_**

Threads: **cheryl_lawson_**

Goodreads: search **Cheryl Lawson**

Acknowledgements

Thank you to my beta readers who helped immeasurably in developing this story. A big thanks to Jodi Christensen for editing Ghost of Time. A special thanks to David who's endless support and encouragement are the reasons why this book even exists. Your support means the world to me.

And lastly, thank you readers for enjoying my stories and supporting my journey as an author.

Cheryl